Vampire Shift

(Kiera Hudson Series One)

Book 1

Tim O'Rourke

D0325212

Story Editor (Hacker)
Lynda O'Rourke
Book cover designed by:
Carles Barrios
Copyright: Carles Barrios 2011
Carlesbarrios.blogspot.com
Copy edited by:
C.J Pinard

For Lynda, who kept on at me to write this...

More books by Tim O'Rourke

Kiera Hudson Series One
Vampire Shift (Kiera Hudson Series 1) Book 1

Vampire Wake (Kiera Hudson Series 1) Book 2

Vampire Hunt (Kiera Hudson Series 1) Book 3

Vampire Breed (Kiera Hudson Series 1) Book 4

Wolf House (Kiera Hudson Series 1) Book 5

Vampire Hollows (Kiera Hudson Series 1) Book 6

Kiera Hudson Series Two
Dead Flesh (Kiera Hudson Series 2) Book 1

Dead Night (Kiera Hudson Series 2) Book 2

Dead Angels (Kiera Hudson Series 2) Book 3

Dead Statues (Kiera Hudson Series 2) Book 4

Dead Seth (Kiera Hudson Series 2) Book 5

Dead Wolf (Kiera Hudson Series 2) Book 6

Dead Water (Kiera Hudson Series 2) Book 7

Dead Push (Kiera Hudson Series 2) Book 8

Dead Lost (Kiera Hudson Series 2) Book 9

Dead End (Kiera Hudson Series 2) Book 10

Kiera Hudson Series Three
The Creeping Men (Kiera Hudson Series Three) Book 1

The Lethal Infected (Kiera Hudson Series Three) Book 2

The Adoring Artist (Kiera Hudson Series Three) Book 3

Werewolves of Shade

Werewolves of Shade (Part One)

Werewolves of Shade (Part Two)

Werewolves of Shade (Part Three)

Werewolves of Shade (Part Four)

Werewolves of Shade (Part Five)

Werewolves of Shade (Part Six)

Moon Trilogy

Moonlight (Moon Trilogy) Book 1

Moonbeam (Moon Trilogy) Book 2

Moonshine (Moon Trilogy) Book 3

The Jack Seth Novellas

Hollow Pit (Book One)

Seeking Cara (Book Two) Coming Soon!

Black Hill Farm (Books 1 & 2)

Black Hill Farm (Book 1)

Black Hill Farm: Andy's Diary (Book 2)

Sydney Hart Novels

Witch (A Sydney Hart Novel) Book 1

Yellow (A Sydney Hart Novel) Book 2

The Doorways Saga

Doorways (Doorways Saga Book 1)

The League of Doorways (Doorways Saga Book 2)

The Queen of Doorways (Doorways Saga Book 3)

The Tessa Dark Trilogy

Stilts (Book 1)

Zip (Book 2)

The Mechanic

The Mechanic

The Dark Side of Nightfall

The Dark Side of Nightfall (Book One)

The Dark Side of Nightfall (Book Two)

Unscathed

Written by Tim O'Rourke & C.J. Pinard

You can contact Tim O'Rourke at

www.kierahudson.com or by email at

kierahudson91@aol.com

Chapter One

My name is Kiera Hudson. I'm twenty-years-old and employed by Havenshire Police as a police constable in the southwest of England. I have been a police officer for eighteen months. On completion of my initial training, I was posted to the coastal town of The Ragged Cove. I'd heard rumours that the post was a difficult one to fill. Although this posting wasn't forced upon me by my superiors, they did make me an attractive offer I found difficult to refuse. The terms of my posting to the town, The Ragged Cove, included free accommodation and an unsociable shift allowance of £5,000, paid in a lump sum annually.

When I told my fellow recruits I had accepted the offer, some of them laughed nervously, stating that the force paid the shift allowance annually as no one had lasted long enough in the post to collect it. My shift pattern was a constant series of nightshifts that started every night at 1900 hours and finished at 0700 hours the following morning. Looking back now, I can understand the raised eyebrows of my friends, but at the time, I didn't want to refuse the post. I thought if I did, I would be viewed as inflexible by my superiors and I had ambitions way past the rank of constable. Like me, most of the other recruits were young, and knowing The Ragged Cove was pretty remote and miles from the nearest railway station or motorway, I suspected they were more concerned about their social lives than their future careers.

So, packing a suitcase, which consisted mainly of my smart new uniform, I set off in my tired, old Mini and headed from my rented room in Havensfield to the desolate town of The Ragged Cove. I remember that day clearly as I made my way by a series of deserted country lanes towards the town. A few miles out, the sky clouded over and it started to rain. The day almost seemed to turn to night, as the rain lashed against the windscreen of my car and the wipers had trouble keeping the screen clear. With my headlights on full beam, I cautiously navigated my way towards the town. Several times I had to pull over off the narrow roads and park up by the entrance to some field and check the map I'd been given by Sergeant Phillips at training school.

I knew the town was remote, but it was only as I tried to reach it that I realised how isolated from the outside world it really was. It seemed to me that The Ragged Cove didn't want to be found. Realising I was just spooking myself, I shook off any regrets I might have been having, and carried on through the rain and gloom.

In an attempt to lighten my spirits, I turned on the car radio, hoping to find something I could sing along to. I settled for *On the floor* by Jennifer Lopez. The roads seemed to get narrower as I headed down towards the cove, which spread out below me like a giant horseshoe. Wiping the mist from the windscreen with the back of my hand, I could see the sea in the distance and it looked black and angry as it crashed against the cliffs. As I neared the town, the radio began to hiss and spit with static until I lost the signal completely. I made the rest of my journey in silence.

I reached the town just before five, but the sky was so dark that it seemed much later. Driving my car through the cobbled streets, I peered up at the tired-looking buildings that lined each side of the road. There was a row of shops which had been shut for the day, and the streets were so deserted, I wondered how they managed to stay in business. Sergeant Phillips said that a room had been rented for me above an Inn named "The Crescent Moon", but I couldn't seem to find it. Over and over again, I drove up and down the same streets, the wind and the rain hammering my little car. Then, just ahead, I saw a lone figure shuffling along the pavement ahead of me. I slowed the car, bringing it to a halt. The engine rattled and rain bounced off its red bonnet. Winding the window down, I peered through the gap and called out to the figure that walked stooped forward, a dark hood pulled up over its head.

"Excuse me," I called out, my breath forming tiny clouds in the cold.

The hunched figure, stopped dead in its tracks, back still facing me.

I tried again. "Hello?"

Slowly, the figure turned on the spot, the hem of the long coat it wore trailing in the deep puddles that filled the cracked pavement. Two gleaming eyes stared at me from beneath the hood. I drew a sudden breath in surprise at the wizened looking face peering out of the shadows beneath the hood. It was difficult for me to guess the man's age, as his face was a network of deep groves and wrinkles. His skin was white and fleshy where the wrinkles hung loose like sacks of skin beneath his eyes. The corners of his thin bloodless lips were twisted in what looked like a painful grimace. But even though his face looked worn and old, his eyes were sharp and keen, shining a brilliant blue from beneath his hood. He continued to stare at me and say nothing.

"I'm looking for a place called The Crescent Moon Inn," I said, inching the window closed so only the smallest of gaps was left for me to speak through.

Still staring at me from beneath his hood, the stranger raised one gnarled finger and placed it against his cracked lips. "Shhh!" he almost seemed to hiss. Then, lowering his head, he turned away and continued to shuffle forwards along the street, rain dripping from his hood.

I closed the window and from the safety of my car, I sat and watched the stranger until he had disappeared into the gloom ahead. Once I was sure he had gone, I started my car again and crept forward. I reached the end of the street, slowed and looked left and right. I couldn't see him in either direction. It was like he had vanished. Indicating right, I turned into yet another narrow, cobbled street, where the houses and shops stood crammed next to one another. It was then,

I noticed that same hooded figure watching me from the darkness of a nearby shop doorway. Looking front, and goose flesh crawling over my skin, I sped up.

It was just before six when I noticed a small side street that I hadn't seen before. Turning into it, my car bounced and lurched over the cobbled road until in the distance, I could just make out the glow of a blue lamp attached to the front of a white-washed building. Any anxiety I had early felt disappeared upon seeing it. I knew I'd found the police station where I had been posted to. They would be able to point me in the right direction to my lodgings, and it would give me a chance to meet with some of my colleagues before I started my first nightshift the following evening.

Parking the car just outside, I pulled my jacket tight about my shoulders and ran towards the old, wooden door below the blue lamp. Pushing against it, I stumbled into the station and out of the howling wind and driving rain. I must have looked a right sight, my black hair matted in dark, wet streaks to my forehead and cheeks, my face pale with the cold.

"Can I help you?" someone asked me.

Looking up, I could see a small front counter. Sitting behind it was a police officer. He had short, grey hair and was clean-shaven. He was about forty-years-old. He was dressed in his uniform and was sucking on an old-looking pipe, which pumped clouds of blue smoke into the air.

"Can I help you?" he asked again.

Straightening my hair and pulling it from my

face, I smiled and said, "I'm Kiera."

He looked back at me as if he didn't have the slightest idea as to what I was talking about. Holding out my hand for him to shake, I stepped towards the front counter and said, "I'm Kiera Hudson. The new recruit?"

Again he looked at me as if I were speaking in a foreign language. Lowering my hand, I added, "Force headquarters sent me. I'm to be stationed here."

Then with a sudden look of recognition on his face, he stood up and came towards me. It was then I noticed he wasn't in full uniform at all, but was wearing a pair of jeans and carpet slippers. He appeared to lean to the right as he walked, as if he had a limp.

"Hudson," he said, thumbing through some paperwork on the other side of the counter. "Hudson. Kiera. Oh, yes," he said, plucking my file from beneath a mountain of paperwork. Then, looking back at me, he said, "You know you're getting old when the new recruits look younger than your daughters."

Noticing the three stripes on his shoulders, I asked, "Are you in charge here?"

Placing my file to one side, he smiled back at me and said, "Kind of, but not really. I'm Sergeant Murphy – 'Murphy' to my friends," and thrust out his hand. Taking it, he pumped my arm up and down until I thought it might just fall off. "We do have Chief Inspector Rom, but we don't see him much. He pops his head in from time to time and that's the way we like it. Don't want the boss nosing around," he said, winking at me as he puffed on his pipe again.

Knocking the fringe from my eyes, I noticed Sergeant Murphy was wearing a small tiepin which was in the shape of a crucifix. I thought this was a little odd as we'd had it instilled in us at training school that we were only to wear police insignia on our uniforms – nothing else, especially not anything that was religious or might cause offense.

Sergeant Murphy saw me looking, and his fingers went straight to it. "I know what you're thinking," he said. "Straight from training school where you've had your head crammed full of all the things you should and shouldn't do."

"No," I said, shaking my head, not wanting to offend my new sergeant in the first few moments of meeting him.

"Well, let me tell you something, little lady," he said leaning over the counter towards me, his voice dropping to a whisper. "This little cross here will offer you more protection than any can of CS spray, a baton, or a Taser. They don't mean diddly-shit in The Ragged Cove."

"Don't listen to the old fart," someone said from behind me.

Spinning round, I saw another police officer step into the station out of the rain. His raincoat dripped water all over the floor, and it ran from the brim of his helmet. Taking it from his head, he shook the rain off. Unlike Sergeant Murphy, this police officer was younger, no older than twenty-two. He had short, black wavy hair, green eyes, and a handsome face.

17

"I'm sorry?" I asked, taken aback by his sudden presence. His jaw line was sharp and square and he had such a deep cleft chin that it looked as if it had been made with a nail gun. Although he was clean-shaven, the lower half of his face was shadowed where black stubble hid just beneath the surface.

"I said, take no notice of the old fart,'" he smiled, looking over my shoulder at Sergeant Murphy.

"You show some respect,'" Murphy said, but he didn't sound angry, it was as if it were a joke he shared with this officer.

Taking off his black raincoat and draping it over the counter, he turned to me and said, "I'm Luke Bishop." Then smiling, he added, "The one who does all the work around here."

"You don't know the meaning of the word," Sergeant Murphy scoffed, going back to his seat where he propped his slippered feet up onto his desk and sucked on his pipe.

"So you must be Constable Hudson?" Luke asked.

"Kiera," I replied, shaking his hand.

"Good to meet you," Luke said, and I couldn't help but notice that he held my gaze just a little too long – long enough to make me feel uncomfortable. Looking away, I noticed the sign above the counter that read:

It is against the law to smoke anywhere on these premises.

Then, looking over at my new sergeant with the

18

pipe dangling from his mouth, he winked at me again and picked up some of the paperwork that littered his desk.

I was immediately struck by the lack of professionalism
Sergeant Murphy showed, and it felt at odds with the almost military-style of policing instilled in me at training school.

"I thought you started your shift with us tomorrow night?" Luke said, cutting into my thoughts. "You're a night early," he smiled, and it was a smile that seemed to light up his whole face.

"I can't find my digs," I told him.

"Where are you staying?" he asked.

"'The Crescent Moon Inn,'" I said, and I couldn't help but notice the look that passed between Luke and Sergeant Murphy across the counter.

"Is there something wrong?" I asked.

Shaking his head, Luke said, "No, there's nothing wrong. I'll show you where it is." Throwing on his overcoat again and grabbing his helmet, I followed Luke outside. As I swung the police station door closed behind me, I could just see the top of Murphy's head on the other side of the counter.

"Welcome to the sleepy town of The Ragged Cove, Kiera Hudson. I'll see you tomorrow night at seven for the start of your first vampire shift."

Not knowing what he meant, I let the door swing shut and I stepped out into the rain again.

"Is this yours?" Luke asked, looking at my beat

up old Mini. "Yeah, why?" I asked, feeling proud of my little red car.

"Nothing." Luke grinned, going to the passenger side.

Opening my door, I got in. Throwing his helmet into the back, Luke wedged himself into the front seat. His legs were so long that his knees seemed to rest just beneath his chin. Smiling to myself, I put the car into gear and we rumbled off up the street.

We sat in silence, and I felt uncomfortable. "So where is this Inn?" I asked, trying to make conversation.

"It's a mile or so up the road from here. Just take a right at the top," he said.

"So what's with the crucifix and all this stuff about starting my first 'vampire shift' tomorrow night?" I asked above the sound of the wipers as they squeaked back and forth in the rain.

"Oh, that's just the sarge trying to be funny," Luke said, staring straight ahead into the dark.

"I don't think he was trying to be funny. It was as if he were trying to give me a warning," I told him.

Glancing sideways at me, Luke said, "Look, some strange things have happened here in the last few years or so, that's all."

"What do you mean by *strange*?" I asked him, struggling to see in the dark.

"Well, apart from some of the new recruits that have been sent from headquarters going missing, we've also had our fair share of grave desecrations and murders for such a small town," Luke said, looking back into the night.

"What do you mean by *missing*?" I asked, feeling intrigued rather than scared.

"Well, they don't show up for work. One day they're here and the next they're gone. Not even so much as a goodbye," Luke explained.

"What, they ask to be posted someplace else?" I asked.

"No, they just go missing," Luke said, and again he looked at me. "I guess they just leave the force altogether. Perhaps they realise that being a police officer isn't like watching cops on the T.V. and they quit and go find something else to do."

"But why?" I asked, slowing down to steer the car around a rather sharp bend in the road.

"Dunno – maybe they weren't expecting so much paperwork,'" he shrugged.

"But you can't have that much paperwork out here," I said. "It can't be that busy."

"You're right," he said. "We don't have a burglary problem, robbery problem, or even that much antisocial behaviour. But like I said, we do have a murder problem, and they create mountains of paperwork."

Speeding up again, I asked, "So how many murders are we talking about?"

"Well if you exclude the thirty or so people that have gone missing, as no one really knows what's happened to them, we've had about twenty murders in the last three years or so."

21

"*Twenty*?" I gasped, nearly crashing the car into a nearby hedgerow. "Some cities in the UK don't even have that amount in five years – let alone a small little town like this!"

"They started slow at first," he explained. "The first year we had three and a couple of disappearances. In the second year we had six murders – but this year they've escalated at a frightening rate."

"Are they connected?" I asked, still reeling from what he had just told me.

"The M.O. is the same in each case, if that's what you mean," he said.

"So you have a serial killer in The Ragged Cove?" I asked him, not being able to comprehend what he was telling me. How my colleagues had been dumb enough to turn down a posting like this was beyond me. Some officers could wait a lifetime before they came anywhere close to even getting a whiff of a serial killer case and here I was right in the middle of one, just days out of training school.

"I don't think it's the work of a serial killer," Luke said, glancing at me again.

"But you said the M.O. was the same in each murder," I reminded him.

"It is the same," he said, then added, "but there is more than one killer."

Gripping the steering wheel so tight that my knuckles glowed white through the skin, I asked, "How can you be so sure?"

"There are always more than one set of prints

at the scene and the…" he trailed off.

"And what?" I asked, almost ready to pee in my pants.

"Forensics say the tooth marks come from different sets of teeth," he said.

"*Tooth marks*?" I almost screeched.

"Yeah, tooth marks," Luke said in a grim tone. "At first we thought they were the tooth marks of an animal because -"

Luke was suddenly interrupted as the airwaves radio attached to his coat began to talk in the sound of Sergeant Murphy's voice.

"Echo One to Echo Three, receiving?" and his voice came through, mixed with the sound of static.

Speaking into the radio, Luke said, "Go ahead, sarge – what you got?"

"I hate to be the one to tell you this," Murphy's voice crackled back over the radio, "but Farmer Moore reckons his dog has just come across the remains of the Blake kid who went missing a couple of days ago."

Taking a deep breath, Luke seemed to gather himself together, then said into the radio, "Okay, sarge, I'll make my way straight there." Then looking at me he said, "Fancy starting your duties a night early?"

"You bet," I told him, my stomach beginning to buzz with nerves and excitement.

"Okay then," Luke smiled, "Welcome to your first vampire shift."

Chapter Two

Luke directed me along a narrow coastal road, and above the sound of the rain and the wind, I could hear those black waves crashing into the cliffs below. At one point, a gust of wind took hold of my tiny car, and I felt the pull of the back wheels as they headed towards the cliff edge. Gasping out loud, I yanked on the wheel and straightened the car. Luke sat beside me and said nothing, his face white and drawn-looking.

As we cleared the coastal road, Luke pointed in the direction of a narrow track and I followed it. At the top, there was a gate which led into a field. Killing the engine but keeping the headlights on, we climbed from the car. Waiting at the gate for us was a short man with a curved back. He stooped forward and used a stick to support himself. He wore a cloth cap pulled so far down his face; it was difficult to see his eyes. Yapping about his heels was a black and white collie.

"Evening, Constable," the man said.

"Good to see you, Moore," Luke said, and the two men briefly shook hands. Moore glanced up at me from beneath the rim of his cap. His ancient face was specked with what looked like festering sores and a cluster of white whiskers covered his chin. Without taking his eyes off me, he said to Luke, "Who's the girl?"

"This is Constable Hudson," Luke said. "A new recruit, fresh out of the box."

"I wonder how long she'll last?" Moore asked, and as he spoke I could see that where once he'd had teeth, there were now a set of fleshly gums.

"Where's the body?" Luke asked, pulling a torch from his utility belt and switching it on.

"Up beyond that treeline," Moore said, waving his stick in the general direction of a crop of trees that lined his fields. "I'm warning you though, the kid don't look pretty."

Flashing his torch towards the trees, Luke said, "You wait here, Moore." Then looking back at me, he said, "Ready?"

Pulling the collar of my jacket around my throat, I nodded. I didn't know if I were ready or not. I'd seen dead bodies before during some cases I had investigated with the help of my friend and colleague Tom Henderson, while still at training school. But thankfully, I had never seen the dead body of a child before. I pushed those memories of those previous mysteries and my friend Tom Henderson from my mind and followed Luke. We made our way across the fields towards the trees. The earth was sodden, and my trainers squelched in the mud. At one point, my foot got stuck and I thought I might just lose my shoe. Pulling me free, Luke took me by the arm and guided me across the field.

Stepping beneath the canopy of trees, the rain seemed to ease, trapped by the leaves above. Shining his torch on the ground ahead of us, Luke went deeper into the crop of trees. It was eerily quiet and I could hear the sound of my own heart thumping in my ears. Without warning, Luke dashed ahead, shouting over his shoulder, "Look – over here!"

I followed, and as I did, I could just make out the shape of something lying face-up in the damp undergrowth beneath the trees. From a distance it looked like a pile of rags, but as I got nearer, I could see that it was the body of a small boy. He was dressed in shorts and a T-shirt which had been ripped open down the front. Luke waved the torchlight up and down the body of the boy. His face looked white and bloated but it wasn't that which sickened me; it was the look of fear forever engraved upon his small face. I had never seen the look of such terror before, and I shivered at the thought of what his attacker must have looked like.

Bending down, Luke got onto all fours, and for a moment, blocked my view of the boy. He seemed to be examining him.

"It's definitely Henry Blake," Luke said.

"How can you be so sure?" I asked, hunkering down beside him.

"Had dealings with the boy before," Luke said. "Nothing serious – just chucking stones and being a nuisance, that's all."

It was then, as I knelt beside Luke, that I saw the injuries to Henry Blake's throat – or what was left of it. From just beneath his chin to his chest plate, the flesh was missing, ripped and torn away in jagged chunks.

Covering my mouth with my hands, I lurched to

one side, desperate not to be sick on my first night and not in front of Luke.

"Are you okay?" Luke asked, looking at me. I could see the concern in his eyes.

"Sure," I said, swallowing hard to push away the bile that was burning the back of my throat.

"If you need a moment..." Luke started and put his arm out to rub my back.

Knocking it away, I stood up and tried to regain my composure. "I reckon he died about three days ago," I said, trying to sound like a police officer instead of some emotional wreck.

"How do you know that?" Luke asked me. And by the tone of his voice, he sounded as if what he really wanted to say was, "How would you know anything? You've only been a cop five minutes!"

"See those blisters,'" I said, pointing to the yellowing bubbles on the boy's arms and legs.

"What about them?" Luke asked.

"Notice how the body is swollen and bloated?" I asked him.

"So?" Luke came back at me.

"And that fluid which has leaked from his mouth, nose, and ears?"

"What are you trying to say?" Luke asked.

"They're all things that happen to a body about three days after death," I told him. "Although I could be a day out, it all depends on how warm the weather has been."

"What's that got to do with anything?" Luke

asked, looking at me.

"The whole process of the body bloating like that can be sped up, depending on how hot the environment is," I told him.

Smiling at me he said, "Where did you learn all that stuff?"

"My dad used to be a pathologist," I told him.

"*Used to* be?" he asked.

"He died recently – cancer," I said.

"Sorry to hear that."

"Me too," I said, looking down at the mutilated boy stretched out before us. "My dad was always telling me all kinds of weird stuff about bodies and things. It was kind of gruesome but it always fascinated me."

"What else can you see, Sherlock?" Luke said, smiling.

Taking the torch from him, I cast light over the scene. "The boy was brought or carried here," I said.

"How can you tell?" Luke asked with a frown.

"Look at his trainers," I told him. "There's no mud. If he walked here, there'd have to be mud, right?"

"I guess," Luke said.

"But wait a minute," I whispered, kneeling down again and checking the ground around the boy's body. I traced the tips of my fingers over the earth and dead leaves then inspected the boy. "That doesn't make sense," I said.

"What doesn't?" Luke asked, sounding confused.

"The boy was murdered here – look, you can

28

see the ground is spattered with his blood."

"So what's the problem?"

"Apart from the boy, there were three others," I told him. "All of them were adults. Two were male, the third was female. The first male was about six-foot-two, the second shorter, about five-ten. He smoked Marlboro cigarettes, Lights in fact. But he came before the others. He had been waiting for them, I guess anywhere between one and two hours. The female was about five-six and had black hair which was dyed blonde."

"Are you making all this shit up?" Luke asked from behind me. "You know, just because you're new to the job, you don't have to try and impress me."

"Shhh," I said, not taking my eyes off the ground. "But there's something wrong."

"What?" he started to sound impatient.

"They can't all have been carried here," I said, more to myself than him. "I can understand them carrying the victim here, but..."

"But what?" Luke hissed from behind me, and he sounded pissed off.

"Look, you can see the ground around the body is covered with footprints," I said.

"Yeah, so?" Luke said, leaning over my shoulder.

"Well, there are no footprints leading to or from the body," I told him.

"And your point is?" Luke asked.

"So how did the killers get here if they didn't

29

walk?" I said, sounding exasperated. "Did they fly?"

Then, before Luke or even I could answer my own question, there was the sound of people approaching us from the distance.

"Who's there?" Luke called out, sounding spooked.

"It's just me and Constable Potter."

Aiming Luke's torch in the direction of the voice, I could just make out two figures approaching us. As they drew nearer, I could see one of them was Sergeant Murphy by the way he stooped to the right and the other I guessed was Constable Potter. He was tall and lean, with black hair that was slicked back off his forehead. He looked slightly older than Luke and I guessed he was about twenty-four-years-old. Both Murphy and Potter had torches, the lights bouncing off the trees.

Reaching us, Sergeant Murphy leaned over the body of the boy and showered him with torch light. "Jesus wept!" he gasped, kissing the tiny crucifix pinned to his tie.

"It looks like we've got ourselves another one," Potter groaned, popping a cigarette between his lips and lighting it.

"I don't think you should be smoking here," I said before I could stop myself.

Raising an eyebrow with a cigarette dangling from the corner of his mouth, Constable Potter looked at me and said, "And you are?"

Before I could answer, Murphy had cut in and

said, "This is Kiera Hudson, our new recruit."

Drawing on the end of his cigarette, Potter smiled at me and asked, "Do you have a problem with me smoking?"

Meeting his stare, I said, "No, but I just don't think you should be smoking here – after all it is a crime scene. At training school -"

"...they fill your head with shit," Potter cut in. "This is the real world, sweetheart."

I was just about to tell him that I wasn't his sweetheart when Luke said, "Kiera says that there was three of them and that the boy has been here at least three days."

I don't think Luke said this to embarrass me, I think he really was impressed with what I had told him.

Blowing smoke out of his nostrils, Potter laughed and said, "Looks like we got a right little Miss Marple this time around."

Eyeing Potter, Sergeant Murphy said, "Okay, Sean that's enough. Let's hear what the girl's got to say."

At first I didn't say anything, fearing Potter would start ragging on me again. I know that I'd only just met him, but I already disliked the guy.

"Go on, Kiera, tell them what you told me," Luke said, and he sounded supportive, like a good friend would.

"Go on, Hudson," Sergeant Murphy urged. "You're with friends here."

So, pointing the torch back at the body of Henry

Blake, I crouched down and started to point out the footprints, blisters, and fluid which had come from the boy's mouth, nose, and ears. Before I'd finished, Potter had started to spray laughter into the darkness.

"What a bunch of horseshit!" he cried. "I don't know what they've been teaching you at training school but whatever it is, you ain't in no episode of *CSI*."

Standing, I looked at Luke and felt embarrassed, wishing I hadn't said anything.

When Potter had stopped laughing, he flicked his cigarette away into a nearby bush and Sergeant Murphy stepped towards me.

"I admire your enthusiasm, Kiera, but Sean is right, this ain't no T.V. program, this is real life. Being a police officer in the real world ain't like what you've been watching on T.V."

Although Murphy was trying to comfort me, I couldn't help but feel he was patronising me.

"I haven't been watching -" I started.

"Kiera, this is a well-walked route by hikers and ramblers. Those footprints could have been left here by anyone. So what if there aren't any tracks leading to and from the murder scene? As far as we know, it could have been a really hot day and the earth could've been as dry as a bone."

I wanted to tell him that in the cool shade of the trees, it was very unlikely that the ground would've been rock-hard, but I knew there was little point. He didn't want some newbie coming into his town and telling him how to do his job. So, however much it pained me, I kept quiet.

I was damp from the rain and cold. Not being able to hide my shivers any longer, Luke approached me, and wrapping an arm about my shoulders, he said, "C'mon, let me get you to your room."

Without any resistance, I let Luke guide me away from the mutilated body of the boy. As I went, I looked back to see Potter lighting up another cigarette. Looking at me, he smiled and blew a cloud of smoke up into the night. I watched the smoke rise upwards, and as it dispersed, I noticed something. Aiming Luke's torch up into the trees, I could see the branches above the boy were snapped and broken as if someone or something had crashed through them.

Turning away, I let Luke lead me to my car. Ten minutes later, I was pulling up outside the Crescent Moon Inn.

"Is this it?" I asked, looking out of the window at the weary-looking building. It almost seemed to lean to the right, as if at any moment it was going to topple over. The roof was thatched and the windows were lattice in design. Wild ivy climbed over the front of the Inn and up across the roof like a giant, green claw. The windows glowed orange from within and a sign which read *The Crescent Moon Inn* wailed back and forth in the wind.

Swinging open the passenger door, Luke went to climb out, but then stopped. Looking back at me he said, "You weren't making that stuff up back there, were you?"

"No," I replied.

"So how did you figure it all out?" he asked, staring at me again and making me feel uncomfortable. "How did you know how tall the killers were, the fact that one of them had arrived before the others, his brand of cigarettes, and that the female had black hair which she had dyed blonde? You musta been guessing some of that."

"I wasn't guessing," I told him.

"What then? Are you some kind of psychic?" and he half-laughed.

"It doesn't matter," I told him, climbing from the car.

Putting his helmet onto his head and pulling the collar of his police coat up about his neck, he said, "So long, Kiera Hudson. I'll see you tomorrow night at seven."

Then turning towards the Inn, just wanting to get out of the rain, I head towards the door, then stopped. Seeing as I now knew where the Inn was, I should really have offered Luke a lift back to the police station. But as I turned back towards him, I was surprised to see that he had already gone.

Chapter Three

Carrying what little belongings I'd brought with me, I went into the Inn. A crescent-shaped bar stood along the far wall. The Inn wasn't very busy, and those huddled around the small fire and the tables fell into a hushed silence and looked at me. As I crossed the floor to the bar, I could feel their eyes on me. It was so quiet I could hear the wood snapping and crackling as it burnt in the fireplace. I looked across at it and noticed that someone had engraved a five-pointed star into the plaster above the fireplace. Then, in the far corner, I noticed a figure. He sat alone at a table which was lit with a candle and he warmed a glass of whiskey in his hand. The male had a hood pulled so low over his head that it concealed his face. Although I couldn't see his eyes, I knew he was watching me. At first I thought that perhaps it was the old stranger I had first seen on arriving in The Ragged Cove, but his hands were free of wrinkles and the fingers were long and straight, not gnarled and crooked like a bunch of broken twigs.

Trying not to make eye contact with those gathered in the Inn, I reached the bar. I had never felt so uncomfortable in my life, and I wondered why Sergeant Phillips had decided to rent me a room in such a godforsaken place. When I thought I couldn't bear their stares any longer and was just about to pick up my case and run from the place, an elderly woman appeared from a small office behind the bar. White lengths of wispy hair protruded from her head, and her face was haggard and lined with deep, ragged wrinkles. She looked like a corpse that had been warmed up.

"Can I help you?" she asked, her voice sounding weak and broken.

"I have a room booked…" I started.

"Name?" the old woman asked, thumbing through a dusty ledger behind the bar.

"Hudson," I said. "Kiera Hudson."

The woman sniffed, and taking a key from a series of hooks on the wall behind her, she placed it on the bar and said, "Room number two."

Taking the key, I said, "Thank -"

"Top of the stairs and turn right," the old woman cut over me. "Breakfast is between six and seven, and dinner between eight and ten."

Looking at my wristwatch, I could see it had just gone ten. "I don't suppose there's any chance of something to eat?" I asked her.

"Dinner is between eight and ten," she repeated without looking up at me.

"I know, but it's only just a couple of minutes past, so I was wondering -" I began.

"Between eight and ten," the old woman said again, but this time she looked up at me. Her eyes were milky-coloured and clouded with cataracts.

Shrugging my shoulders as if I didn't really care, I picked up my case and as I did, I noticed something rather odd. All the way along the old oak beams that supported the bar, someone had tied reams of garlic bulbs. There were hundreds – no thousands of them. As I looked up, I could see they hung from the ceiling, the back of the Inn door and walls.

"What's with the garlic?" I asked, turning towards the old woman, but she had disappeared back into her tiny office. Turning my back on all those watchful eyes, I made my way up the stairs to my room. Holding onto my case, I fumbled with the key as I slipped it into the lock. Hearing it click, I pushed the door open and shut it behind me. The room was in darkness, so I ran my fingers blindly along the wall in search of the light switch. Finding it, I flipped it on, and the room lit up with a dim bulb that hung from the centre of the ceiling. I looked around my new home and understood why none of the other recruits had stayed a full year in this place.

There was a narrow bed wedged in the far corner, an old fashioned-looking wardrobe, and a desk with a lamp. The carpet looked threadbare, and the walls were a dingy, grey colour. There was a small bathroom, which had a toilet and bath. I didn't know how much headquarters was paying the old woman downstairs, but whatever it was, they were being ripped off.

Placing my case onto the bed, I went to the bathroom and ran myself a bath. While it was running, I unpacked my stuff and hung it in the wardrobe. When I was all fixed up, I got undressed and climbed into the hot water. Closing my eyes, I leant my head back against the rim of the bath. I thought about everything that had happened since arriving at The Ragged Cove and my mind soon wandered to Luke Bishop. Out of everyone I had met so far, he seemed the nicest. He had a kind and honest way about him, and I was grateful he took my side over that of Potter, who seemed like a real prick. Loved himself, too, by the way he was acting all cocky. Sergeant Murphy, I was still to make up my mind about. He seemed set in his ways and I guessed he didn't want some young cop coming in and telling him how to run things. But I wasn't trying to do that. I didn't care that he wanted to lounge around the police station all night in his slippers, smoking a pipe. But what did trouble me was his apparent disregard for properly investigating a crime scene, and not any old crime scene. That was the murder of an eight-year-old child and he was letting that idiot Potter smoke and trample all over it.

If only they'd taken the time to study it, they would have *seen* the things that I had. It wasn't magic – the clues were there if you looked for them. I'd always been like that. My father had called it my 'gift' – but it wasn't really – I just had a knack of noticing things that others seemed unable to see. I saw stuff that other people missed. But it wasn't magic and it wasn't a 'gift', I called it 'seeing'.

But what about Luke? What could I *see* about him? Nothing. He was like a blank sheet of paper. Apart from his obvious good looks and incredible smile, it was the fact that he was a mystery that I found so attractive.

I felt a sudden pang of guilt as I thought of my friend Tom Henderson. Friend? More than a friend? That was over now. It had to be. It was the best thing for both of us. But it hurt to think of him and what he might be doing right now. Was he thinking of me too? Or had he met someone new? A small part of me hoped that he had. I just wanted Tom to be happy and I knew he wanted the same for me too. But for now we had to stay apart. Perhaps one day – in a different time and place – we might be together again. But I was just torturing myself even thinking like that. So, sinking beneath the hot water, I let images of the Blake boy lying dead with his throat ripped out, ripple across the front of my mind as I concentrated on the crime I had been presented with. There were two things that troubled me. My father had often told me that you could tell a lot from a crime scene by the pattern of blood left behind. But that was the problem – there was very little blood for such a gaping wound. The brachiocephalic artery had been ripped apart and I remembered my father telling me once how he had worked on a murder where the victim had had their throat cut. Their life blood had pumped away through the wound in that particular artery.

How then had there been so little blood at the murder scene of the Blake boy? Where had all the blood gone? It was almost as if it had been siphoned off, and what about the lack of footprints leading to and from the scene? I didn't buy Murphy's theory about the ground being too dry for any prints to be left. If prints could be lifted from carpets and lino floors, they could be seen in earth – how ever dry. But how had the killers gotten to the scene? The only clue was the hole made in the trees above, where the branches had been broken and smashed. It was almost as if someone or something had entered the crime scene from above. But that would be impossible, right?

As I tried to examine these theories inside my head, I was startled by the sound of someone outside my bedroom door. Leaping from the bath, I wrapped a towel around me and went into the bedroom. Tiptoeing to the door, I listened to the rustling sound. Screwing up my eyes, I could see a shadow fleeting back and forth in the gap beneath my door.

Reaching out for the key I'd left in the lock, I called out, "Who's there?"

There was silence.

"What do you want?"

Then I heard the sound of footsteps rushing away. Holding the towel tight about me, I yanked open the door and peered along the landing. And as I did, I caught the last fleeting glimpse of a shadow disappearing down the stairs. My instincts told me to run after them to find out who it had been. But with nothing on except the bath towel, I reluctantly stepped back into my room, and as I did, I noticed a small white envelope tacked to the door.

I removed it and went back inside. Across the front of the envelope someone had scribbled 'Kiera'. I sat on my bed, and as I opened it, a small silver crucifix fell out into my hand. Placing it on the desk beside my bed, I went back to the envelope. My heart skipped a beat, as I could *see* from looking at it, that the person I'd seen sitting in the bar with their face hidden behind the hood, was the person responsible for leaving me the crucifix.

Chapter Four

I woke early, just before six. I didn't want to miss breakfast like I'd missed dinner the night before. The owner of the Inn seemed particularly strict on the rules surrounding meal times.

As I pulled on a sweatshirt, jogging bottoms, and trainers, my stomach groaned. It was then I realised I hadn't eaten anything since before leaving my home in Havensfield the day before. As I made my way down to the dining area, I switched on my mobile phone. I scrolled through my contact list, until I came across 'Sergeant Phillips'. I pressed the call button, but all I got back was an unobtainable tone. As I reached the dining area, I noticed the signal bar on my phone was red, indicating that it was unable to find a signal.

Putting the phone in my pocket, I was frustrated that I couldn't get hold of Phillips. I wanted to ask if he could find me some better accommodation. The old woman I'd spoken with the night before trundled over to my table which had been laid with a bowl, plate, and a mug. Apart from me, the small eating area was deserted.

"Tea or coffee?" the old woman croaked, not looking up from a small pad she held in her liver-spotted hands.

"Good morning," I smiled, hoping to get off on a better footing with her than I had the night before.

"Tea or coffee?" the woman asked again, and her eyes met mine with her glazed stare.

"Coffee, please," I told her, trying to keep my smile.

"Bacon and eggs?" the woman asked, the pen poised over her note pad.

"Just toast please." Although I was hungry, I wanted to go for a run and I didn't want to be bloated out with a stomach full of greasy bacon and eggs.

"Toast," the woman said, turning away and shuffling towards the kitchen. The dining area, like the bar, was decorated with cloves of garlic, but with one difference. Along the far wall was a small coffee table which was covered with a white lace cloth. On top were an arrangement of crucifixes and small bottles of water. Someone had written the words 'Holy Water' across each bottle with a black marker pen.

Smiling to myself, as I wasn't superstitious at all, I got up from my seat and crossed over to the table. The crucifixes were identical to the one that had been left for me the night before. Picking up one of the tiny bottles of water, I heard the old woman speak to me as she shuffled towards my table with a plate of toast.

"They're for sale, if you want one." she said, placing the plate on the table.

Putting the little bottle of holy water back with the others, I crossed back to my table and sat down.

"Why would I want to buy a bottle of holy water?" I asked her, and took a bite of the toast.

"For protection," she said, pouring a cup of

43

coffee.

"Protection from what?" I asked, half-smiling.

Glancing back over her shoulder as if she were scared someone might be eavesdropping, she leant in towards me and whispered, "From the vampires," and her breath smelt stale and warm against my face.

Looking straight back at her, I said, "I don't believe in vampires."

"That's what the others said when I tried to warn them," she hushed, snatching another quick look over her shoulder.

"Who?" I asked, sipping my coffee.

"The other ones," she sighed, starting to sound impatient. "The other police officers who came here before you."

Looking into her milky-grey eyes I asked, "Do you know what happened to them?"

"They -" she started but was cut dead by a gruff-sounding voice from the other side of the room.

"That's enough, mother!" the voice said, and I looked up to see a fat, balding man come waddling into the dining area. He wore a red chequered shirt with the sleeves rolled to the elbows and a white apron that was smeared with old food and drink. His cheeks were flushed red and his forehead glistened with sweat.

"The girl has a right to know!" the old woman barked at him.

"There's nothing for her to *know*!" her son snapped back. Then, crossing towards the table with the bottles of holy water and crucifixes, he added, "And

44

how many times have I told you to get rid of all this bloody nonsense?"

"You keep a civil tongue in your head, Roland!" the old woman hissed. "This is still my Inn – it ain't yours yet."

"But you're scaring away all the customers," he told her, his jowls wobbling.

"It ain't me that's scaring 'em off," she snapped at him. "It's those things – those *creatures*!"

Roland saw me staring at both of them as they argued in front of me. With a fake smile stretched across his face, he wiped his meaty hands on his apron and came towards me saying, "I'm sorry about mother. Don't be put off by what she says."

Munching on the last of the toast, I smiled and said, "Don't worry about me, I'm not easily spooked."

Hearing this, the old woman hobbled towards me and leaning into my face she gasped, "You *will* be."

Taking his mother by the arm, he escorted her from the room and back into the kitchen. Within moments, he had returned and came to clear away my empty plate and mug.

"So what is all this stuff about vampires?" I asked him.

"Just stories," he said, without looking at me. "Okay, the town has had more than its fair share of strange goings on, but I don't agree with all this scaremongering. It was good for business at first. People came from all over to visit the town, believing it to be infested with vampires. We did the Inn up as you can see, and we even did a roaring trade in those little crosses and bottles of water, but it was just a laugh, you know, to attract the tourists," he told me.

"So what went wrong?" I asked him.

"More and more murders started to happen. People started to go missing and then there was the grave robbing," he said, wringing his hands together.

"Grave robbing?"

"Yeah, but it was more than that," he said, his voice dropping to a whisper. "The bodies of those poor murdered souls were being dug up and stolen."

"By whom?" I asked him.

"Greedy freaks, that's who," he spat. "The whole thing just started to get out of hand. People were making a lot of money – me included – off the back of the rumours being spread about the vampires. But people got bored or scared of The Ragged Cove, and just stopped coming. The guest houses started to empty, the restaurants had no bookings, and then High Street became deserted. So the incidents just got more and more bizarre, and I reckon it was all down to some of the locals, hoping that they could entice people back by strange evil-doings and stories. Everybody likes a good scare, don't they?"

"I guess," I said. "But digging up the bodies of murder victims seems a bit extreme."

"Not if you've got mouths to feed and a business to keep going," he said. "Folk will do the strangest of things to survive."

"But what about these murders?" I asked him,

interested to see what his view was. Like me, he hadn't been hooked on the whole vampire thing.

"Undoubtedly there is a murderer in our midst," he said, and again his voice had dropped to a whisper. "But I reckon all this attention is just encouraging him, getting him all excited-like."

I didn't tell him about the three sets of tracks I had found by Henry Blake's body. I let him continue to believe the murders were being committed by just the one killer.

"What do you mean 'excited'?" I asked.

"These serial killers love all the attention they get from the media, don't they," he said more as a statement than a question. "Seen it on the T.V. I have. They love it when the newspapers give 'em a name like 'The Ripper' or 'The Black Panther', makes 'em feel all important like – when really, they're nothing but scum," he said.

"So do you have any ideas?" I asked him.

"About what?" he asked.

"Who this serial killer might be," I said, staring at him.

Then, looking straight back at me, Roland said, "Shouldn't I be the one asking you that question? After all, you're the police officer, ain't ya?"

Getting up from my seat, I said, "I'm working on it."

"You make sure you do, pretty lady, 'cos that sergeant of yours couldn't find his own arse with both hands and a flashlight," he said as I reached the door.

Looking back at him, I said, "I'm sure Sergeant Murphy is doing his best." But in my heart, I doubted he was.

Chapter Five

The morning was overcast and dreary, but at least the rain from the night before had stopped. I didn't know the area at all, and I thought I would spend the morning getting to know it. My first official nightshift started at seven, and I wanted to get a feel for the place and its people before I started policing it. If I were going to be successful in my new post, I would have to know my patch.

Heading back in the direction Luke had brought me the night before, I started a slow jog. There were no pavements and I had to keep to the side of the road. In some places, the undergrowth was so overgrown; I had to run further out into the road. It wasn't as if I were putting myself in danger, as the roads seemed deserted. Not one car or person had passed me in the last twenty minutes or so.

Slowing down, I looked left then right, trying to decide on which way to go. Then, looking over my shoulder in the direction I'd come, my stomach tightened and my heart sped up as I saw the hooded figure from the previous night. He was cycling towards me, his face hidden by the same hoodie he'd worn before. Turning front again, I turned left, wondering if he would follow me. I hadn't gone very far when I glanced back again, and to my surprise I saw him turn onto the narrow road I had taken.

I tried to tell myself that perhaps it was just coincidence that he was cycling the same stretch of road I'd chosen to jog along. But who was I trying to kid? He was following me. After all, I knew it had been him who had left that crucifix tacked to my door. But why? Perhaps I should ask him?

Slowing to a standstill in the middle of the road, I turned around. With my hands on my hips, I faced the oncoming hooded cyclist. Seeing I had stopped running, he stopped cycling. There was a long moment that seemed to stretch out forever, as I stared at him while he stared back at me from beneath his hood.

Turning my back on him, I started to run again, this time picking up my speed. After a short time I looked back, only to find he had started cycling again towards me. I slowed and so did he, always careful to keep a good distance between us. What did this guy want? I wondered. And why wouldn't he show his face?

Again, I stopped running and turned to face him. As I suspected he would, the cyclist stopped and just sat and watched me.

"What do you want?" I called out, and my voice sounded echoey as it travelled across the empty fields on either side of the road. "How do you know my name?"

The hooded guy said nothing, but just sat on his bike and looked at me from beneath his hood. Then, without giving him any warning, I ran as fast as I could towards him. He turned his bike around in the road and pedalled as fast as he could away from me.

Knowing I could never catch him, I slowed, doubled-up gasping for breath. Once I had stopped, so did the cyclist ahead of me. Turning his bike again in the road, he sat and watched me.

Drawing in lungful's of oxygen, I shouted as loud as I could, "Why did you leave me that crucifix?"

The cyclist, whoever he was, didn't respond; he just sat motionless on his bike.

"I know it was you!" I yelled at him. Turning, I started to run again. Okay, I thought. If he wanted to play games, I could play along. Ahead there was a bend in the road, and running as fast as I could, I raced towards it. I rounded the bend and saw that it opened out into a wide, open area of wild grass and sand, which led down through the cliffs and towards the cove. Off to the right was an outcrop of rocks. Diving behind them, I lay flat against the ground. From my hiding place, I could hear the sea crashing against the shore in the distance, and the sound of seagulls as they squawked overhead.

Peering around the rocks, I watched as the cyclist rode his bike onto the open area. He stopped, looking from left to right, his hood never moving, not offering the smallest glimpse of who was beneath it. After a few seconds, he rode forward and headed towards the rocks. As he drew nearer, I could see his hands were covered with gloves, and apart from the dark black hoodie, he wore blue jeans and trainers. There was a chill in the air, but I found it odd that he was so snugly wrapped up and wearing gloves. It was as if he didn't want to show any of his skin.

Squatting on all fours, I waited for him to draw level with the rocks. When he was almost on top of me, I sprang from my hiding place and made a desperate grab for his handlebars. I managed to get hold of one before he twisted them away and out of reach. Holding on as best I could, the bike wobbled and the cyclist steadied himself by slamming both of his feet down into the sand.

"Who are you?" I hollered at him, his head lowered so I couldn't see beneath his hood. "Tell me who you are!" I demanded.

Without so much as a murmur, he rolled the bike backwards, dragging me along with him. Losing my footing, I fell forward, letting go of the handlebar. As I went down, I caught my wrist on one of the bike pedals, tearing the skin from my wrist. I cried out in pain, rolling into the sand, cradling my bleeding arm. Seeing he had cast me loose, he pedalled as fast and as hard as he could away from me and back down the narrow lane towards the cove.

"Come back!" I yelled after him, but he was soon gone, disappearing amongst the rocks and cliffs. I rolled onto my back and gripped my bleeding wrist in an attempt to stop the flow of blood. It oozed through my fingers in red, sticky rivulets, and for just the briefest of moments, I felt dizzy and the world seemed to turn black.

"Are you okay?" I heard someone say.

Opening my eyes, I looked up to see Luke

standing over me, a concerned look etched across his face. "What happened?"

"I fell over," I said, trying to get to my feet.

"Come here," Luke said, offering me his hand to help me up. It was then he saw the blood flowing through my fingers and he almost seemed to flinch in horror.

"What's wrong?" I asked, getting myself to my feet. Again, I couldn't help but notice that he seemed unable to take his eyes off the blood which now ran up my wrist towards my forearm. The colour had drained from his face and he looked suddenly unwell.

"Are you okay?" I asked him as he took a step backwards.

Continuing to look at my bleeding wrist, Luke said, "I'm not very good around blood. It kind of makes me queasy."

"You're meant to be a cop," I winced in pain.

"I know, but I just don't like the sight of blood, that's all," he said, and again I noticed that he couldn't help but stare at the cut.

"Well don't just stand there," I said. "Give me a hand."

Shaking his head as if coming out of a trance, he said, "I'm sorry. Sure." He pulled his sweatshirt from over his head and wrapped it tightly around my arm. I noticed how careful he was not to get any of my blood on him.

"What are you doing out here?" I asked him as he knotted the sleeves of his sweatshirt around my arm like a makeshift bandage.

"I could ask the same of you," he said, eyeing me.

"I was taking a run," I told him. "That was, until I started to be followed."

"Followed?" he asked, sounding alarmed. "By who?"

"I don't know," I shrugged. "He had his face covered. But he left me a crucifix outside my room last night."

"A crucifix!" Luke said. "Why?"

"I don't know that either." I told him.

"Where is he now?"

"Cycled off down there after knocking me to the ground," I said, pointing in the direction of the rugged path. "Where did you come from?"

"That way," Luke replied, nodding in the direction I had been pointing.

"You must have passed him then," I told him. "He was on a bike."

Shaking his head, Luke said, "No one passed me on a bike."

"Are you sure?" I asked, feeling confused.

"Sure," he replied. "Now let's get you back to the Inn, before you bleed to death."

"You never said what you were doing way out here," I reminded him.

"Oh," Luke smiled, "I often drive out here, park up, and take in some of the sea views."

"Where's your car?"

"Over there, on a piece of flat," he said, pointing beyond the rocks. "There's a narrow road, but you can get a car up here if you're careful." Then he wrapped his arm around my shoulder and led me back down the path.

Chapter Six

Back at the Inn, I invited Luke up to my room. Luke closed the door behind us and sat on the chair by the desk as I went to the bathroom. I had no worries about inviting Luke into my room, even though he was pretty much a stranger to me. He was a cop just like me, so that had to count for something. Alone in the bathroom, I removed the makeshift bandage from my wrist. I pulled off my sweatshirt and ran my arm under the cold tap. The icy water made the cut sting and I winced in pain.

Luke appeared in the doorway. "Is everything all right?"

Seeing that I was standing there in my bra, the colour suddenly returned to his cheeks. Although he looked embarrassed walking in on me like that, he didn't immediately turn away, but lingered in the doorway, looking at me. I didn't move, either, although deep inside I knew that perhaps I should have. But something and I didn't know what, kept me rooted to the spot. And for the longest seconds of my life we just stood and looked at each other. Then slowly, I covered my chest with my good arm and said, "You couldn't get me a fresh top from the wardrobe, could you?"

There was another pause as if it took a moment for my request to register with Luke. He looked away and almost collided with the doorframe. "Sure. Give me a minute."

Placing my wrist back under the running water, I cleaned the cut with a piece of tissue paper. To my relief, I could see it wasn't deep and thankfully wouldn't need stitches.

"Here you go," I heard Luke say.

I looked up to see his arm poking around the doorframe with a T-shirt hanging from his fist. This time around, he hadn't barged straight in on me. I turned off the running water, patted the cut dry with the tissue, then snatched the T-shirt from him. Pulling it over my head, I went back into the bedroom to find him sitting in the chair by the desk.

"Are you okay?" he asked me.

"I'll live," I told him.

"I'm glad," he said, and flashed me one of his smiles.

Taking some plasters I had buried at the bottom of my make-up bag, I covered the cut. When I had finished, Luke asked, "Had you seen the guy on the bike before?"

"Last night, in the bar downstairs," I told him.

"Then again leaving the crucifix outside your room?" he asked.

"No, I didn't see him do that," I said.

"Then how did you know it was him who left it?"

Pointing to the envelope on the desk, I said, "That was the envelope he left. Look at it. What can you see?"

Picking up the envelope, Luke turned it over in his hands. After several moments, he looked at me and said, "It's got your name on the front."

"But what else can you see?" I pushed him.

With a blank expression on his face, he said, "Nothing."

"Give it to me," I demanded, holding out my hand.

Coming to sit next to me on the bed, Luke handed me the envelope. "The guy I saw in the Inn last night was wearing a hoodie and he wore it in such a way as to mask his face," I told him.

"So if you didn't see his face, how do you know it was him?" Luke asked.

"I'm getting to that," I said. "The guy in the hoodie was sitting at a table in the corner. He was sitting away from the rest of the other people in the bar. The corner of the room was dark and I noticed there was a candle on the table. He was holding a glass of whiskey in his left hand."

"So?" Luke said.

"Well take a closer look at the envelope," I told him, holding it up. "The writing on the front has been written by a man. See the way the writing leans to the right? That suggests it has been written by a left-handed person."

"But that still doesn't mean..." Luke started and leaned in closer to me.

"Now look here and here," I said, pointing to the top right-hand corner of the envelope. "See those spots of wax? He used the candle so he could see to write my name on the front, and in doing so, some of the wax spattered onto the envelope. I had dealt with something similar before while still at training school. It was just a few drops of wax that helped me and my friend Tom catch..."

"But..." Luke tried again.

"Then there's this," I said, lifting the flap of the envelope and running the seal against the tip of my nose. "The unmistakable smell of whiskey. The man probably took a swig to moisten his tongue to seal the envelope securely."

"And the crucifix?" Luke asked, sounding somewhat in awe.

"Easy-peasy," I smiled. "They sell them in the bar."

"But..." Luke mumbled.

"I know, it's all subjective, but I was convinced I was right after my tussle with the man on his bike this morning," I said.

"But how?"

"As I gripped his handlebars, again I noticed several spots of white wax on the sleeve of his black-coloured hoodie. You would've had to been blind not to have seen them." Then, looking Luke straight in the eye, I added, "I know this town is somewhat remote but they do have such a thing as electricity. It seems doubtful, then, that he would have got the wax on his sleeve anywhere other than the bar downstairs."

Luke sat in silence for a moment, then said,

"That's brilliant, Kiera. That was bloody awesome!"

Blushing, I said, "See, I told you it wasn't magic. It's just that I have this ability of *seeing* things that other people don't."

"Is that how you knew so much about what had happened at the crime scene in the woods last night?" Luke asked.

"Yes," I said.

"I still reckon you guessed some of it!"

"I never guess," I told him.

"But how did you know how many killers there were? How did you know what sex they were, the fact that one had arrived before the others and had waited more than an hour for them? And that one of them dyed their hair?" Luke asked, never taking his eyes from mine.

Breaking his stare I explained. "Firstly, there were three different sets of footprints around the body. Two sets were too big to have belonged to females. The third set was much smaller. Too big to be a child's, and too small to be a man's. So that only left a female. By the size of the gait between each footstep, I could roughly work out each person's height. One of the males, the one that was about five-foot-ten tall, was the smoker. His footprints were clearly visible by the tree next to the body of the dead boy. Several cigarette butts, Marlboro in brand, had been ground out by the base of the tree by the same boot that left the footprints, which meant they could have only been left by him and not anyone else. The fact that there were several, suggests that he waited some time for the others, and while he did, he smoked to pass the time. Depending on how heavy a smoker he is, depends on how long he waited there. Let's say he smoked four to five in an hour, then he waited about an hour and a half, but no more than two.

"Wrapped around one of the boy's fingers was a long, blonde hair. It could have come from the head of a male, but after quickly examining it in the torchlight, I could see that the first half inch of the hair leading from the root was black. Therefore, the hair would more than likely have come from the female. It's not often that a male would have dyed his hair peroxide blonde. And that's about it," I finished.

"That's about it?" Luke whistled through his teeth. "You noticed all of that in the short space of time you were there?"

"It just happens," I told him. "I just *see* stuff."

"That's spooky," Luke said.

"No, it's good police work," I smiled. "I haven't told you anything that forensics wouldn't find."

"Forensics," Luke said, and his voice sounded kind of flat.

"I know this town is like at the end of the Earth, but you must have forensic officers?" I asked him.

"Yeah, we do have a forensic officer," he said, sounding as if he were trying to hide something from me.

"Who?" I asked.

"Potter," he said, looking away as if he were

ashamed.

"That cretin?" I exclaimed. "He couldn't find his way out of an elevator!"

"He's been on a course and everything," Luke tried to assure me.

"A course?" I said in disbelief. "No wonder the killers haven't been caught if he's responsible for examining the crime scenes."

"He seems to do a thorough job," Luke tried to assure me. "I've seen him gathering up evidence and bagging and tagging it for SOCO to examine."

"You have scenes of crime officers posted out here?" I asked, hoping that he would say yes.

"No," he said. "But Potter puts the stuff in the freezer back at the station and they either collect it, or he sends it to them via the post."

"And what have been the results so far?" I asked him.

"Not much I guess, or we would have the killers locked up by now," Luke said.

"What about those teeth marks you told me about?"

"We're not even sure what type of creature they belong to. The teeth don't appear to be that of a human, more like some kind of wild dog," Luke said.

"There wasn't any dog or any other type of wild animal involved in the death of Henry Blake," I insisted.

"But even with your great powers of observation," Luke said, "you still don't know how the killers got to and from the crime scene?"

He looked at me and I pictured the broken branches in the trees above the boy's mutilated body.

"Well?" he asked, sounding impatient.

"I don't know," I admitted, the only possibility left after examining the scene was that the killers had entered the scene from above. But I didn't want to say that – because it would have been impossible.

"Look, Kiera, we've lived with these murders for the last few years. And yeah, we might not be super-cops from headquarters, but we've done our best with the limited resources that we have," he said, getting up from the edge of the bed.

Holding out my good hand towards him, I said, "Luke, I wasn't trying to knock you or your team – it's just…"

"Just what?" he asked. "None of us are as switched on as you? Is that it?"

I shook my head and looked away from him.

"You've been in The Ragged Cove five minutes and you think you know this case better than us," he said. "Well let me tell you something for nothing, this ain't a normal town and the murders ain't normal either. Whoever or *whatever* is carrying out these killings will be caught. One way or another, we'll catch them."

"I'm sorry," I said. "I didn't mean to offend anyone."

"Just take some time to get to know this town and its people before you go jumping to any conclusions," he suggested, and his voice had softened.

Then, coming towards me, he took my hand in his. His skin felt cold. Then just like he had in the bathroom, he stared at me.

"I hope you last longer than the other recruits they sent."

"Why?" I asked, looking into his pale green eyes.

"Cos' I like having you around," he smiled. Luke let my fingers slip from his and then headed towards the door.

"Is that the only reason?" I found myself asking him. And I wasn't sure why I was bothered if he wanted me to stay in The Ragged Cove or not.

"And you seem like a pretty good cop," he said, turning to look at me.

"Just *good*?" I grinned back.

"If you really want to impress me," he said, "tell me the name of the hooded guy who's been following you and then explain how those killers got to and from that crime scene. Do that and you won't just be good – you'll be amazing!" Snatching up his sweatshirt which was covered in my blood, he left the room, closing the door behind him.

I went to the window and looked out. After a few moments, he appeared below and made his way to his car. Unaware that I was watching him, he climbed into the front seat. Then he did something so strange and unexpected, I gasped aloud. Taking the sweatshirt, he raised it to his face and sniffed the bloodstains left on it.

Starting the engine of his car, he sped off down the country lane and disappeared from view.

Chapter Seven

I slept to just before six, and when I woke, my room was in darkness. Still wearing my jogging bottoms and T–shirt, I remembered crashing out on my bed after Luke had left earlier. I'd only intended to doze but was grateful that I'd slept well, as I had my first nightshift starting in just over an hour.

Crossing to the window, I looked out at the cold December evening and could see that it was raining again. *Didn't it ever stop raining in this town?* I wondered. After a quick bath, I got dressed into my uniform and went downstairs. Before leaving my room, I snatched up the tiny silver crucifix and stuffed it into my shirt pocket. *For luck,* I thought to myself. As soon as I stepped onto the landing, I could smell roast beef wafting up from downstairs. The smell of it made my stomach somersault with hunger, but I didn't have time to stop and eat, I'd have to grab something later while out on patrol.

As I made my way down the stairs, I pulled my mobile phone from my pocket. The signal bar was still glowing red, telling me there was no reception. I was still keen to contact Sergeant Phillips – if nothing more than to update him to how I was settling in. As I passed through the bar area, the old woman was shuffling back and forth behind it.

"Do you have a phone I could use?" I asked her.

"Phone?" she said.

"Yeah, I need to make a call and don't seem to be able to get a signal on my mobile," I told her.

"Sure we have a phone," the old woman said.

"Do you think I could you use it please?"

"You could if it worked," she said, eyeing me with her glazed stare.

"What's that supposed to mean?" I asked her. "Is the phone broken?"

"Not broken," she cackled. "This god-darn weather we've been having has brought down all the lines in the area. God only knows why we even bother to pay for line rental in these parts. They're always coming down."

Looking into her watery eyes, I said, "Not to worry, I'll use the phone at the station."

"Good luck, dear," she half-smiled as I turned away.

Throwing my hat and utility belt onto the passenger seat, I made the drive to the police station. As it had the night before, rain and wind lashed against my tiny car and I gripped the wheel, hoping I could keep it on the road. Leaning forward, I switched on the radio and was met with the deafening sound of static. Switching it off, I sat back in the seat and began to feel that the world outside The Ragged Cove was fast disappearing.

Parking my Mini outside the station, I grabbed my kit and hurried inside. Sergeant Murphy was sat as I'd found him the night before, slippered feet propped up on his desk, pipe dangling from the corner of his mouth. Potter was on the other side of the desk and was filling out some paperwork, a cigarette smouldering away in an ashtray in front of him. Again, I looked at the *No Smoking* sign fastened to the wall. Potter caught me looking at it and he just grinned at me.

The door leading from the front office opened and Luke stood on the other side of it.

"Evening, Kiera," he smiled.

"Hello, Luke," I said, and thought of how I'd seen him sniffing the sweatshirt with my blood on it.

"You okay?" he asked me.

"Sure," I said.

"It's just that you look a bit apprehensive," he said.

"First night nerves," I smiled back.

"You've got nothing to be nervous about," Sergeant Murphy said. "We're one big family here."

"I'll show her where everything is," Luke said.

"No, Potter can show Kiera around," Murphy suddenly said. "I've got a report that has just come in that I need to discuss with you."

With a cigarette smouldering from the corner of his mouth, Potter pushed his chair back from the table and stood up. I wasn't overjoyed at the thought of having to spend any time with Potter, but then again, was he any worse than Luke? Luke seemed friendly and easier going, but then again I thought I'd caught him smelling my blood on his sweatshirt earlier that day. With something close to a scowl on his face, Potter hooked his thumb in the direction of a door set into the far wall of the outter office.

Leading me into a narrow corridor, cigarette smoke trailing back over his shoulder, Potter pointed out the female bathroom and locker room, the mess room, and exhibits store. At the end of the corridor was a secured cabinet. Taking a key from his pocket, Potter said, "You'll need one of these."

He took one of my hands in his, and pressed the key into my palm. His touch was ice cold, like he had just pulled his hand from beneath a stream of cold running water.

I pulled my hand quickly away at his touch. A grin formed at the corner of his lips and his dark eyes shone mischievously. I closed my fist around the key and broke his stare.

"The key will open the cabinet where we store the CS spray and Taser," Potter told me. "Yours are marked with the number four."

"What's under there?" I asked him, pointing to a hatch in the floor of the corridor. It had been secured with a large padlock.

Potter dropped the cigarette end to the floor and squashed it flat with the sole of his boot. He lit another almost at once. "You don't need to worry about what's down there," he said in a patronising tone. "That's just the basement. It's full of old office furniture and stuff – just crap,"

Taking me by the arm, and steering me away from the hatch in the floor, he led me further down the

69

corridor. I pushed his hand away. From the corner of my eye, I saw him smile to himself, as if he were part of some private joke but only he knew the punch line.

At the end of the stone corridor was a metal gate. Unlocking it, Potter swung it open and said, "This is the cell area. There are only three cells. We don't have much use for them. But they do come in handy from time to time."

Switching off the light, he swung the gate shut. "Get your stuff together and I'll take you out on patrol," he said.

"But I thought I was going out on patrol with Luke…" I started.

"Looks like our first night will be a busy one," someone said over my shoulder.

I glanced around to find Luke standing behind me. Grateful that he had saved me from having to spend any more time with Potter, I said, "How come?"

"Sergeant Murphy has just informed me that Father Taylor, the priest up at St. Mary's, has reported that another grave has been desecrated," he told me.

"Who's grave?" I asked him.

"The grave is that of a fifteen-year-old girl who was killed a month or so ago. Her name was Kristy Hall," Luke said.

"How did she die?" I asked, already guessing his answer.

"Like the others – throat ripped out," he said, turning away. "I'll see you outside in five."

Drawing my equipment from the secured

cabinet, I couldn't help but feel Potter's eyes boring into me as he stood smoking and watching me take a radio that had been charging in the office. Trying my best to ignore him, I put on my police jacket. The guy made me feel uncomfortable.

Looking up from his paperwork, Sergeant Murphy said, "All set, Constable Hudson?"

"I guess," I said, fastening my jacket.

"You be careful out there," Potter smirked, sucking on the end of his cigarette.

"Don't take any notice of him," Murphy said. "I'm sure Bishop will take good care of you. He's a good lad. Bit naive, but a good lad."

"Taking you up to the graveyard, is he?" Potter grinned.

"That's right," I said.

"Keep an eye out for the vampires," he said, and again that cheesy grin of his spread right across his face.

"Vampires?" I asked, as if I had no idea of the stories I'd already been told.

"Haven't you heard?" Potter said with mock surprise.

"Heard what?" I said, acting dumb.

"Put a sock in it," Murphy told Potter. Then, turning to face me, he added, "Just be careful, Kiera, and you'll be fine."

I turned my back on them and left the station. Luke was waiting outside in a marked police car. I yanked open the passenger door and jumped inside, throwing my cap onto the back seat.

"Good?" Luke asked.

"Oh yeah," I said, glad to be back in my uniform and raring to go.

"Let's get going then," Luke smiled back at me as we sped into the night towards the graveyard at St. Mary's Church.

We drove in silence and I couldn't help but think back to how I'd seen him smell the bloodstains on his sweatshirt. So to break the uncomfortable silence and to find out a little more about him, I said, "So what's your story?"

"You tell me," he said, looking straight ahead. "You're the super sleuth," and I caught him smiling.

"That's the problem," I said. "You don't give much away."

"Work your magic," he said over the sound of the wiper blades.

"You're not married," I told him. "You don't have a girlfriend and you live alone."

"How can you be so sure?"

"No wedding ring for starters," I smiled.

"But I could live with a girlfriend," he said back.

"No, I don't think so."

"What makes you so sure?"

"You use cheap smelling soap and no aftershave, so you're not trying to impress anyone. You hurriedly ate a fried egg sandwich before you left for work tonight, which suggests that you can't cook and there isn't anyone cooking for you, so therefore you live alone. The sweatshirt you lent me today hasn't been washed since you last had a haircut, which I'm guessing was about four weeks ago by its current length. Again this suggests you're a typical bloke fending for himself and only having to do a wash when you really need to. You haven't had a female in your car – apart from me – in the last six months. So everything added together, tells me that you're single and you live alone," I told him.

Luke smiled at me and said, "Very good. I can see now how you figured some of it out. But how did you know what I had for my dinner, that I hadn't washed my sweatshirt since my last haircut, and the fact that I haven't had a female in my car for over six months? Sadly, it's been a lot longer than that, but how did you know?"

Looking out of the passenger window and into the dark, I smiled to myself and said, "You have ketchup and egg on your tie and some down the front of your trousers, which wasn't there last night. When you lent me your sweatshirt earlier, I noticed that around the neck there were hair clippings, which tells me that you were wearing it the last time you went to the barber and as the hairs are still there, you couldn't have washed it. As for the car thing? There is an oily-black thumb print on the vanity mirror in your car, probably left by the mechanic who last serviced it. If you'd had a woman in there, she would've wiped it off so as to check her make-up from time to time. In the foot well of your car, along with a load of other rubbish, I noticed a receipt from the garage where you last had the car serviced, which was dated six months ago."

"Jesus, you don't miss a trick do you?" he said. "I can see I'm going to have to be careful around you."

Looking at him, I said, "Why? Have you got something to hide?"

Before he could reply, Luke was slowing the car. "Here we are," he said.

Looking through the windscreen, I could just make out the tall steeple of a church set back from the road in the middle of a graveyard. Tall, leafless trees wrenched back and forth in the wind, like dark twisted limbs. Just looking at the place gave me the creeps and I shivered.

Grabbing my cap from the back seat, I climbed from the car and out into the driving rain and howling wind. The graveyard was surrounded by an ancient-looking stone wall. Luke led me around it, bent forward against the wind. Reaching an old weather-beaten gate set into the wall, Luke pushed it open and we made our way through the gravestones to the front of the church. The wind was bitterly cold, and the rain jabbed at my face like needle points.

Then without warning, someone stepped from the shadows of the church and said, "Rather inclement weather we're having."

Without being able to stop myself, I yelped at the sudden appearance of the figure.

"I'm sorry, my child. I didn't mean to scare you," the man said. On his head, the stranger wore a wide-brimmed black hat and rain ran from it in constant rivulets. His face was thin and gaunt-looking as if he were sucking in his cheeks. His eyes were bright and keen and they almost seemed to twinkle in the darkness. His lips were thin, and twisted upwards in a grim smile. Beneath the upturned lapels of his long black coat, I noticed the white markings of his clerical collar.

"Good evening, Father," Luke said with an awe-like respect.

"Good evening, Constable Bishop. I'm so glad that you and...?" he looked at me and gave that grim smile again.

"Constable Hudson," I said, over the roaring wind.

"Constable Hudson," he said, and his eyes twinkled again as he looked me up and down "Very good."

"Sergeant Murphy said you'd left a message – another grave has been disturbed?"

Nodding his head and leading us towards the back of the graveyard, he said, "Yes, sadly so, Constable. God rest the poor soul. Only fifteen-years-old was poor Kristy. It doesn't seem more than a few weeks ago that I was baptising her as a baby."

He led us further away from the church into the darkest corner of the graveyard. I pulled my torch from my belt and switched it on. Weaving the beam of light before me, I could see rows and rows of gravestones, stretching out in every direction. Some leant to one side, others looked smashed or broken. The inscriptions on some had either worn away or had been covered by moss.

"This way," Father Taylor said, leading us towards a tall tree that twisted up into the night sky like a giant ogre. As we drew near, Luke switched on his torch, and with both our beams of light, I could see a mound of disturbed earth ahead of us. With my heart racing in my chest and my stomach tightening, we made our way towards it. Once we were a few feet from the broken and disrupted soil, Father Taylor stopped.

"What's wrong, Father?" Luke asked.

Crossing himself, he looked at us from beneath the brim of his hat and said, "I can't go on, Constable. There is evil at work here tonight." And he crossed himself again.

"Evil?" I asked him.

Ignoring me, Father Taylor spoke to Luke again. "I'd be better served back in my church, praying for the soul of that poor girl." Then looking at the both of us he added, "I shall pray for you too."

Without another word, the priest turned and hurried back off into the night, back towards the church, which loomed like a shadow in the distance.

"I guess we go on alone," Luke said looking at me.

I stared back at him.

"Are you sure you want to go on?" he asked.

"Don't concern yourself about me," I said, trying to mask my nerves. "I'll be just fine."

I brushed past him. Reaching the grave, I shone my torch into the hole in the ground. Luke came to stand beside me. The rain made a drumming sound against what was left of the coffin lid. It was splintered and ripped open. Crouching down to get a better look, I could see that the coffin was empty – the body of Kristy Hall had been taken. A putrid stench wafted out of the hole, and I covered my nose and mouth with my free hand.

"What can you see?" Luke asked, kneeling beside me.

"Not a lot," I said, shining my torch over the walls of the grave and the ground surrounding it. I placed the end of the torch between my teeth and I swung my legs over the side of the grave.

"What are you doing?" Luke asked, gripping my shoulder.

Taking the torch out of my mouth, I said, "Getting a better look."

"Are you insane?" he asked; rain running down his face like tears. "Can't it wait till daylight?"

"Not in this weather," I told him. "The rain will wash away any clues that might be left." I bit the end of the torch again and scrambled into the open grave.

"Hang on!" Luke shouted over the howling wind. But it was too late. I was gone.

I landed with a thump on top of what was left of the coffin lid. Wiping rain from my eyes, I pulled back the lid and some of it came away in my hands. The coffin was lined with white silk, which was now wet and soiled. Maggots and spiders scurried away, frightened back into the darkness by the light from my torch.

Inside the coffin I found a small toy bear, obviously buried with the girl by her parents. Her favourite toy to accompany her on her journey to wherever it was she was going. Steadying myself in the slippery mud, I placed one hand against the wall of the grave and bent forward. There was something glistening in the corner of the coffin. Balancing on the broken coffin lid, I reached down and picked it up. Holding it up in the torchlight, I could see it was a string of rosary beads. I placed them back where I'd found them and pulled away part of the coffin lid, turning it over in my hands. In doing so, I saw something that almost stopped my heart and made my blood run cold.

The underside of the coffin lid was covered in claw marks. There were no marks on the top like there should have been if someone had broken into the coffin. But to my horror and disbelief, they were underneath. The lid was covered with them, and how ever improbable, the only conclusion I could come up with was that Kristy Hall had been buried alive and she had raked and clawed at the underside of the coffin lid as she tried to get out. Dropping the piece of wood, I shone my torch around the walls of the grave and could see similar claw marks in the earth, as if she had scrambled out.

Numb with shock at what I'd discovered, I looked up at the hole above me.

"Luke, you won't believe this!" I shouted.

There was no answer, just the sound of the rain thumping down at me and the wind screaming above.

"Luke!" I called out, this time louder. "Luke, are you there?"

No answer.

"Luke!" I called again. And this time I detected a tremor of fear in my voice and I hated myself for it. Where could he be? Perhaps he had gone back to the car to get some evidence bags so we could do the job properly for once?

Realising that he wasn't coming back in a hurry and just wanting to be out of the grave, I switched off my torch, fastened it to my belt and started to scramble up the inside of the grave. The earth was wet and slippery and several times I lost my footing and slid back down on top of the coffin again.

"Luke, goddammit," I cursed under my breath, and started to climb again. As I neared the top, I saw a shadow of what looked like a person flit past the opening above me.

"At last!" I muttered. "About time you came back." I said, pulling myself from the hole. I was filthy. I had wet mud all over my hands, down the front of my jacket and trousers, and my boots were caked with the stuff. I turned around, expecting to see Luke, and jumped with such a start that I nearly toppled back into the grave. Standing just a few feet away from me was a teenage girl.

Fumbling for my torch, I yanked it from my belt and shone it at her. Immediately, the girl threw her hands to her face and screeched as if in pain.

"I'm sorry," I said, wanting to scream myself.

I looked at the girl and I could see she wore a filthy dress. I guessed it had once been white; but it was now covered with earth and dirt. Her hair was long and matted in filthy clumps to the side of her ashen face. Her fingernails had earth beneath them and her bare feet and ankles were splashed with mud.

"Are you okay?" I asked her, not knowing what else to say. I was still stunned by her sudden appearance in the graveyard.

"Mummy," she said. "Where's my mummy?" and her voice sounded deep and hollow.

Starting to back away, I reached for my radio, wanting to call for Luke.

The girl came towards me, her steps long and slow.

"Kristy?" I said, fumbling for my radio. "You are Kristy, aren't you?"

"I want my mummy," she said again. "I'm hungry." And she sniffed the air and licked her lips with a dry-looking tongue.

"I'll find your mummy for you," I told her, leaning my head towards the radio.

Sensing I was going to call for help, she reached for my radio with one filthy hand. I could see that her fingers were long – more like claws. Stumbling backwards, I yelled into my radio, "Luke if you're receiving this, I need backup right now!"

The radio crackled and hissed, and the girl

covered her ears. She screamed as if the noise was unbearable. Then over the sound of the wind and the rain, I heard a tearing noise. It sounded wet and moist, like flesh being ripped from bone. The girl jerked backwards and her back arched. Rolling her head back on her shoulders, she opened her mouth and screeched as if in agony.

Her whole being seemed to ripple and contort in front of me and I shouted into my radio again.

"Luke! Luke! I need urgent assistance right now!"

Again, there was only static.

The girl lowered her head and looked at me. Her eyes glowed like hot coals as if they were on fire. She opened her mouth and her two front incisors were now long and razor-sharp. She came towards me, and for a moment, I seemed unable to move, captivated by her frightening beauty.

All the while she moved towards me, working her way between the gravestones, her hair now billowing in the wind. The girl rolled her shoulders back as if shrugging and I could hear her bones twisting and stretching beneath her skin. The sound of it shook me from my trance. Focusing on the creature that was approaching me, every survival instinct I had was screaming at me to *run*!

Spinning around, I raced as fast as I could away from the girl. My legs felt like jelly. I willed them not to buckle beneath me and send me crashing to the ground. Weaving my way between the rugged gravestones, white plumes of breath squirted from my nose and mouth and disappeared into the cold, black night. Behind me, I could hear the sound of feet fast approaching. Not being able to help myself, I glanced back over my shoulder to see the girl within reaching distance. She pounced into the air.

Dropping to the ground, I rolled over onto my back to see the creature go soaring over me. Realising she had missed, the girl landed and came rushing back. She moved at an incredible speed, her hair billowing out behind her like a mane. Kristy's hands looked like talons, and she grabbed for me. Taking a deep breath, I rolled away, her claws snagging at my jacket. Not daring to look back, I got to my feet and ran towards the gate in the wall. With my heart feeling as if it were going to burst in my chest, and my arms working like pistons by my sides, I ran for my life.

Reaching the gate, I yanked it open. Sliding over the bonnet of the police car, I pulled open the door and climbed into the driver's seat. Hitting the automatic lock with my fist, I screamed into my radio one last time.

"Luke! Luke! I need urgent assistance. *Please help me!*"

Nothing.

Finding the key swinging in the ignition, I turned it and the car rumbled into life. Gripping the steering wheel, I looked ahead to see the girl pouncing out of the night sky straight towards the windscreen. Throwing the car into reverse, I started back down the narrow lane. But she was too quick. Within an instance, the creature had slammed into the windscreen. Cracks started to appear in the glass, spreading out like a spider's web. Punching her long talon-like fingers into the bonnet of the police car, they cut through the metal like it was made of cardboard. Throwing her head back, Kristy smashed her face repeatedly into the already-cracked windscreen. It broke, showering me in splinters of glass.

"Get away from me, you bitch!" I screamed, throwing the gear stick into drive. The creature shot forward, her head coming through the hole in the glass, her razor-sharp teeth snapping just inches from my face. Foam flew from them and spattered me. Slamming down on the brake, the girl flew backwards off the car and crashed into the stone wall that circled the graveyard. I shot forward too, my face smashing into the steering wheel. My nose started to gush blood and I could feel it hot and sticky as it ran over my lips and off my chin.

With my head pounding, I looked up to see the creature lying stunned on the ground against the wall. Stamping on the accelerator, I shot the car forward, my plan to crush her against the wall with the front of the police car. But just before striking her, she looked up, saw the danger she was in and sprang away into the dark. With no time to react, the front of the police car crumpled against the wall. I shot forward in my seat. Sticking out my arms, I managed to absorb much of the impact. Screaming in pain, I heard a thud as something landed on top of the car.

Looking up, I could see the roof begin to buckle inwards as the creature pounded her claws into the top of it. Dazed and confused, I tried to focus as I searched for the emergency lights and sirens. Finding the right switch, I punched it and the night lit up in strobes of luminous blue and red. The sirens started and above them, I heard the sound of screaming. Twisting in my seat, I looked out of the window and upwards, to see the creature, her claws pressed against her ears.

Seizing the moment, I threw the car into reverse again and could have yelled in joy, as despite the damage to the car, it rumbled into life and started to roll backwards. With one hand on the wheel, and looking back over my shoulder, I tried to call for help again.

"Luke! Luke!" I shrieked into my radio. "If you can hear me – please, I need you!'"

Nothing.

With the night sky throbbing blue and red and the *whoop! whoop!* sound of the sirens breaking apart its silence, I raced the car backwards, the monster wailing and banging above me. I found a gap in the road and spun the car around so it was facing away from the church and back towards town.

I pressed as hard as I could on the accelerator. Blood continued to gush from my nose and it tasted coppery in my mouth. With the back of my sleeve, I wiped it away, and as I did, I saw Kristy scrambling from the roof of the car and onto the hood. With her eyes burning red and her mouth wide open in a scream, she launched herself at me through the broken windscreen. Losing control of the car, it crashed into a ditch, stopping dead in its tracks, lifting me from my seat and bashing my head against the roof. Everything started to turn black, and I fought to stay conscious, knowing that if I didn't, I would be dead. Climbing onto the crumpled bonnet, the girl crawled towards me.

"Keep away from me," I cried, reaching for my Taser. Then, at the very last moment, changing my mind, I stuck my hand inside my jacket.

"Hungry," the girl hissed, climbing into the car via the broken windscreen. Licking her lips with a bright red tongue, spit swung from her jagged teeth.

I looked into her eyes, and they seemed ablaze, as if her brain were on fire.

"Hungry!" she screeched, lunging forward.

"Suck on this!" I screamed, stabbing the tiny silver crucifix into her tongue. Almost at once, the girls eyes grew fat and wide and the brightness within them seemed to fade. Throwing her hands to her mouth, she gagged as if choking on glass. White foam began to ooze through her fingers, her mouth frothing like a rabid dog. Shrinking back from me, Kristy slid down the bonnet as if being dragged by her ankles. Screaming, a gush of milky-looking liquid shot from her mouth. It splattered over the bonnet of the car, blistering the paint. Covering my eyes with my arm, I watched as she shot backwards into the sky, disintegrating in an explosion of ash and dust.

Sensing the danger was over, I leant back in my

seat. My chest was pumping up and down as I tried to gasp in air. Every part of me trembled, adrenaline racing through my body. Then, just when I thought it was all over, I heard the sound of footsteps racing towards the car. Glancing into the wing mirror, I could see a pair of black booted feet coming towards me. With trembling fingers, I reached for my Taser, but as everything around me started to fade, I lost consciousness. The last thing I saw was Luke's terrified face looking in at me through the shattered car window.

When I woke, it was dark. I was lying on something soft. Although I felt disorientated and confused, I knew that someone was close. "Who's there?" I asked, my voice sounding croaky.

"It's me, Luke," he said.

"Where am I?'"

"Back in your room."

My head hurt and my face felt bruised. "Am I okay?" I asked, feeling drowsy.

"You'll be fine," he said from the darkness. "Just some cuts and bruises. You were in a nasty car crash."

"It was a car crash?" I mumbled, consciousness fading again. "There was a vamp -"

"Shhh," he said, moving away. "We can talk about it tomorrow."

"Don't go," I whispered.

"What?"

"Stay with me," I said. "I don't want to be alone." I had spent my life *seeing* things, but now when I closed my eyes, all I saw was the terrifying face of a vampire screaming out of the darkness at me.

"Why?" he asked coming back across the room towards the bed.

"I don't want to be alone," I told him. I thought I had got used to feeling lonely since me and my friend Tom had taken separate paths, but the sense of loneliness I now felt was crushing. "Don't go, Luke," I whispered again.

Without saying anything at all, Luke climbed onto the bed next to me. Wrapping my arms around him and resting my head against his chest, I shivered against his cold embrace. I slipped back into unconsciousness.

Chapter Eight

It was light when I woke. Dull, grey sunlight seeped in through my window, making my room look like an old black and white photograph. My head felt sore, as did my nose, and my mouth felt as if I'd been sucking on sandpaper all night. I was lying on top of my bed in just a T-shirt and knickers and I wondered how I'd gotten here and who had undressed me. Then I remembered Luke had been in my room last night and a vague image of me holding him came flooding back. Blushing, I pulled the blankets over me and called his name. I couldn't see him, but the bathroom door was closed and I wondered if he might be in there.

Getting no reply, I swung my legs over the side of the bed, wincing at the pain inside my head. In fact, my whole body ached and throbbed and I felt as if I'd been in a car wreck. Then as if being punched in the face, the memories of what had taken place the night before came rushing back. Like a waking nightmare, I could remember everything. Climbing into the open grave, finding the scratch marks on the underside of the coffin lid, Luke disappearing and not answering my calls on the radio, the girl, Kristy Hall, turning into a vampire and chasing after me as I tried to escape in the police car. Shuddering, I remembered how I had stabbed the crucifix into her tongue, then watched her explode in a pile of dust.

Had all of that really happened? In my head, I tried to tell myself that it couldn't have, but in my heart I knew that it had, and the realisation made me want to throw up. Hobbling to the bathroom, I knelt over the toilet and heaved. Once I'd been sick, I leant against the bath. What was happening to me? What was happening in The Ragged Cove?

Feeling bruised and battered, I turned on the taps and started to fill the bath with warm water. Shuffling back into my room, I searched for my mobile phone. Holding it up into the grey dawn light, I groaned at the sight of the red signal bar flashing on the screen.

"What is wrong with this place?" I hissed. "It's like it's shut off from the rest of the world."

I desperately wanted to call Sergeant Phillips and tell him what had happened to me and what I'd seen. Whether he would believe me or not, I didn't know. But I needed to tell him that all was not well in the sleepy town of The Ragged Cove.

The town seemed to exist in its own little universe. None of the telephones worked, the police radios didn't seem to transmit – even my car radio didn't want to pick up a signal. Realising that I hadn't actually listened to any music since my radio went dead in my car two days ago, I pulled my iPod from my case and took it with me into the bathroom.

Easing myself down into the water, I stretched out. Closing my eyes, I popped the earphones into my ears and turned on the iPod. Rihanna started to sing 'Only girl in the World'. I did feel like the only girl in the world – the *world* I now found myself trapped in.

Closing my eyes, I turned the volume up and rested my head against the back of the bath. Over and over again the memories of what had happened the night before kept playing out in my mind. Could those murders have been committed by vampires? But weren't they just in movies and books? If I hadn't been attacked by one, then I would have said yes, but now I wasn't so sure. Was the boy, Henry Blake killed by them? But that sort of thing just didn't happen. Like my father had been, I was only interested in facts. But I could remember him telling me that once you had studied all the evidence and had dismissed all the theories and rumours, whatever you were left with, however unlikely, was the truth.

Okay, so let's just say that the murders and disappearances were the work of vampires – who were they? Did they live among the townsfolk by day and kill by night? Were they all gathered together in some secret location? And how many were there?

With so many questions racing around my mind, my head began to hurt all over again. But there was one question that just wouldn't go away: Where had Luke disappeared to last night? Where had he been when I'd needed him?

Climbing from the bath, I toweled myself dry and brushed my teeth. Pulling on a pair of jeans, T-shirt, and jumper, I tied my hair into a ponytail and checked out the cuts and bruises on my face in the bathroom mirror. I had a green-blue bump on my temple, my top lip was spilt and I had a graze just beneath my chin. What with the gash on my wrist, I'd never had so many cuts and bruises in such a short space of time.

With my stomach aching for food, I decided to try out Roland's bacon and eggs. Toast this morning just wouldn't be enough. Opening the door to my room, I found another envelope tacked to it. As before, 'Kiera' had been scrawled across the front. Pulling it free, I opened it to find another tiny silver crucifix. Looking at the envelope, I could see that it had been left in the last couple of minutes or so. Yanking the door closed behind me, I ran down the stairs, through the lobby, and out into the road. I looked left, and then right but the road in both directions was deserted. Although I knew he had left the envelope only moments before I'd discovered it, what I didn't know, was how he knew I needed another crucifix.

Chapter Nine

Taking a seat at one of the tables in the small dining area of the Inn, the old woman made her way around the nests of tables and chairs.

"Looks like you've been in a fight," she said, eyeing the cuts and bruises on my face.

"I'm okay," I said, forcing a smile.

"It ain't right," she said, pouring me a mug of coffee.

"What isn't?" I asked.

"A pretty girl like you being a cop 'an all."

"How's that?" I asked, kind of flattered by her remark.

Then looking over her shoulder as if being spied on, she turned to me and said, "If you're not careful, you'll end up dead...*or worse*."

"What could be worse than being dead?" I asked her, sipping the coffee.

"One of the living dead," she whispered, and her voice sounded dry and raspy.

Looking into her cloudy, grey eyes, I was just about to ask her to tell me more, when Roland appeared in the doorway that led from the dining area and into the kitchen.

"Mother!" he hollered, and the old woman seemed to flinch at the sound of his voice. "How many times have I told you not to go upsetting the guests with your stupid stories?"

Before turning to face her son, the old woman slipped her hand into her apron, removed something, and gave it to me. Then winking, she said, "That's on the house." Before I had a chance to say anything, she shuffled away.

Uncurling my fingers, I could see that she had slipped me one of the tiny bottles of holy water I'd seen the previous day.

Hiding it beneath the table, I watched Roland come towards me. His beefy face looked hot and tired. "I'm sorry about that," he blustered. "Mother doesn't know when to stop talking."

"It's okay," I assured him.

"What can I fix you up with?" he asked, wiping his greasy hands on his white apron. Although I felt a little sickened by the sight of his lack of hygiene, my stomach continued to rumble.

"Bacon and eggs would be good," I told him.

"Bacon and eggs it is," he smiled, turning away.

As he wobbled back across the dining room, I called after him and said, "I don't suppose you've seen a guy hanging around here this morning?"

Turning to face me, Roland said, "I don't think so. What did he look like?"

"I don't really know," I told him. "He wears a hoodie so it's kind of hard to see his face."

"Haven't seen anyone like that," he said. "What did he do?"

Taking the envelope from my pocket, I held it

93

up and said, "He left this tacked to my door about five minutes ago."

"How do you know it was in the last five minutes? It could've been left at any time." he said.

"The seal is still damp from where he licked it," I told him.

"Oh," said the fat little man, shrugging his shoulders.

"Don't suppose you have any CCTV, do you?" I asked.

"CC what?" he asked.

"Never mind," I told him and drank my coffee.

Despite Roland's greasy hands and apron, the bacon and eggs were wonderful. The bacon was crispy and the scrambled eggs were light and fluffy. After breakfast, I wrapped up warm and drove my car into town. I wanted to get a better feel of my surroundings and pop into the police station to speak with Sergeant Murphy about what had happened the previous night.

The day was bitterly cold, but the rain had stopped at last. The sky looked like a layer of bruised skin, as dark purple clouds covered the sun. Turning on the car's heater, I warmed myself as I navigated the narrow, winding roads. As I reached town, I couldn't help but notice that the streets and shops were pretty much deserted. I only passed a handful of people, their heads down, as if too scared to make eye contact with anyone. Parking my car in front of a small Post Office, I walked the length of the small high street towards the police station. There was a tea shop, and a couple of old people gathered around a table out of the cold. I passed a shop that sold walking and hiking equipment, but a CLOSED sign hung in the window and the lights were out. There was a fishmonger, butchers, and green-grocers, but none of them seemed very busy, and again I wondered how these little shops made any money.

Turning off the main high street, I made my way up the small cobbled side road towards the police station. Reaching it, I pushed against the door and was surprised to find that it was locked. Standing on tiptoe, I peered through the small front window. The station was in darkness. Biting my lower lip, I wondered why the station wasn't open. Didn't they have a dayshift on duty?

"You won't find anyone on duty at this time of day," someone said from behind me.

Spinning round, I found an elderly gentleman walking his dog. The black-coloured Labrador was taking a leak up a nearby lamppost.

"What did you say?" I asked the man.

"They only seem to work at night," the man said. He looked as if he were in his mid-sixties. He was on the scrawny side, with a wrinkled face and short, white beard. His eyes were a piercing blue. On his head he wore a flat cap, and in his hand he carried a walker's cane, which had a distinctive silver top. He wore a green wax coat, tweed trousers, and a worn pair of hiking boots. Without even knowing that I was doing it, I could tell he was a heavy smoker, he liked a good drink, and he wore glasses to read. At some time in his life, he had been a military man and had served in the parachute regiment. He was returning from a walk along the beach, not the woods, and he was going to have sausages for his dinner, some of which he would probably share with his dog – not with his wife – she was dead and had died recently.

"Don't you know it's rude to stare?" the elderly gentleman asked me.

"I'm sorry," I said, but I couldn't help notice the dark brown nicotine stains on the first two fingers of his right hand, the deep red capillary veins on his cheeks, the pinch marks on either side of the bridge of his nose left by his glasses, the winged crest of the parachute regiment pin attached to the lapel of his jacket, the sand covering the tips of his boots, cane and the paws of his dog, the pack of sausages protruding from his coat pocket and the black armband strapped around his left forearm. Sometimes I wished I didn't have to *see* all these things. Why couldn't I just look at someone like any ordinary person would? My father called it a 'gift' but I often thought of it as a curse. Sometimes my head felt like it was going to burst with all the information that my eyes absorbed.

"Like I said, young lady, you won't find any police on duty at this time of day," the old man said. "If you want to report a crime, come back then."

"Okay, thanks," I said.

"Visiting are you?" he asked, eyeing me with suspicion. "You're not a reporter, are you?"

"Why would I be a reporter?" I asked, feeling

96

bemused.

"Come to spread lies about what's been going on in the town?" he said.

"'What's been going on?" I asked.

"Well if you don't know, then let's keep it like that," he said, and whistled for his dog to catch up with him. "What you don't know can't hurt ya."

He whistled again, but his dog seemed reluctant to come towards us. "C'mon, you daft thing!" the man spat.

The dog cowered by the lamppost and made a whining noise in the back of its throat. "Come here I'm telling ya!" the man ordered his dog. But again it whined, like it was scared of something.

"What's got into ya?" he asked, walking back towards the animal.

Taking hold of the dog by its collar, he dragged it towards the police station. As they got near, the dog began to bark and howl. I watched the man struggle with his pet, as it dug its claws into the street, not wanting to come too close to the police station.

"Stop messing about, you stupid thing," the old man shouted and slapped the dog's hind quarters. Again, the dog howled as it was dragged nearer to the station. Then, as the old man succeeded in drawing the dog level with me, it started to snarl. Why was the dog snarling at me? Its lips rolled back from its teeth in anger – or was it fear? It was like the dog could sense something within me that it didn't like or feared. Looking back at the empty building, I could only wonder what had upset the animal so much.

With a struggle, the old man managed to get his dog past the station and almost at once the dog seemed to calm down. Glancing back, the old man said, "So long, pretty lady. Whatever your business in The Ragged Cove is, leave as soon as you can." Then releasing his dog, he followed it away and out of sight.

I pushed against the locked door of the police station one more time, then made my way back to my car. Sitting behind the wheel and strumming my fingers on the dashboard, I thought about what the old man had said. Why weren't there any police officers on duty during the day in The Ragged Cove? Then, realising I knew very little about my colleagues, I wondered where they went, where they lived, and what they did in such a small town when not on duty.

Outside the Post Office, I noticed a public telephone box and it gave me an idea. I climbed from my car, and I yanked open the heavy red door. I lifted the receiver and wasn't surprised to find the line was dead. But it wasn't the telephone I wanted, it was the telephone directory. Taking it from beneath the phone, I thumbed through it until I got to the letter 'M'. How many Murphy's could there be in such a small town as this? Running my finger down the list, I couldn't find one Murphy listed. I then looked under 'P' for Potter, but again there wasn't anyone with that surname living in town. Drawing a deep breath, I turned to the letter 'B' and just like the others, there wasn't anyone with the name Bishop listed, either.

Stepping out of the phone box, I went into the Post Office. By the door, there was a stand that contained postcards. Taking the first one that came to hand – I really didn't care what picture was on the front – I wrote this message.

Dear Sgt Phillips,
I believe I'm in great danger in the Ragged Cove. I don't want to leave my post – but please come. Your help and advice urgently needed.
Police Constable Kiera Hudson.

I quickly scribbled the address of Police Headquarters onto the card and bought a stamp from the postmistress. Taking it from me, she placed it into a sack that hung on the wall behind her. Leaving the Post Office, I went back to my car and drove away As it was still early, I decided to go back to the church. I wanted to examine the open grave in daylight – I needed to know if there was anything that I'd missed and anything that might lead me to the vampires, if that's what Kristy Hall had really transformed into. Not only that, I wanted to have my facts straight for when I returned for my nightshift. I suspected that Sergeant Murphy would want a full account of what had happened.

Following the winding roads out of town, I managed to find my way back to the church. Parking just down the road from the front gate that led into the graveyard, I climbed from the car. The day had turned bitterly cold, and I thrust my hands into my coat pockets. My fingers brushed against the bottle of holy water and the crucifix and I hoped I wouldn't have to use them again so soon.

As I approached the wall circling the graveyard, I could see flecks of white paint where I'd crashed the car. The gate wailed on its rusty hinges as I made my way into the graveyard. I weaved through the gravestones and although it was day, it took nothing away from the creepiness of the place. As I made my way deeper into the graveyard towards the overhang of the trees in the corner, I could see two people standing by the desecrated grave I'd climbed into the night before.

Crouching, I ducked behind a gravestone and peered into the distance. One of them was the priest, Father Taylor, and the other I couldn't quite see. Darting from my cover, I raced towards another gravestone and snuck behind it. From here, I had a better view of the second person. Looking at them, my stomach began to knot and my mouth turned dry. Father Taylor was deep in conversation with the hooded man who'd been following me and leaving crucifixes outside my bedroom door. Shifting my position behind the grave, I strained to see his face beneath the hoodie. But however much I tried, it was dark beneath the trees, and the overcast sky only made it more difficult to see him. I was too far away to hear what they were saying to one another. From my hiding place, I watched them talk. Several times the hooded man pointed into the open grave.

After only a few minutes of spying on them, they shook hands, and Father Taylor walked away. And as he did, I noticed that he was limping. He hadn't done so the night before – I was sure of it – I would have *seen* it.

Making myself as small as possible, the priest walked right past me on the other side of the gravestone that I was crouching behind. I watched him go back towards the church. Turning back to spy on the hooded male, I watched him kneel down and carryout some kind of an inspection of the earth around the open grave. Taking a small bag from his jacket pocket, he scooped up some of the earth and placed it inside the bag.

As I watched, part of me wanted to sneak up on him, pull back his hood and find out his identity. But what if he saw me before I could reach him? I'd already had a confrontation with him and come off worse for it. So I decided to wait for him to finish whatever it was that he was doing, then follow him. After all, he knew where he could find me and it would be nice to be on equal terms. I didn't have to wait long before he turned away from the open grave and started back across the graveyard.

Peering over the top of the grave, I watched him go to the front of the church, where he disappeared from view. Scrambling to my feet, I darted amongst the gravestones, desperate to catch up with him. As I neared the front of the church, I saw the male speed out from the other side on his bike and cycle down the path to the gate. On reaching it, he leant forward, pulled it open and maneuvered through it and was gone. A thought occurred to me and I froze. To get back down the road, he would have to cycle past my car. He would know that it was mine – how many other beat-up old red Minis were there in the town?

Keeping as low as possible, I made my way towards the wall. Peeking over it, I could just make out my car parked further down the road next to the hedgerows. I couldn't see the cyclist. Passing through the gate, I made my way towards my car. Once I was sure he wasn't nearby, I ran towards it, wanting to catch up, so I could follow him from afar and see where it was he was headed.

Climbing into my car, I started the engine and turned on to the road. Hitting the accelerator, I drove back towards the town, scanning the road ahead for the cyclist. After a mile or so, I'd hoped that I would have seen him ahead of me, but it was like he had vanished. Glancing in my rear view mirror, I hit my brakes. He was tailing *me* on his bike. Not believing what I was seeing, I pulled over and stopped, but kept the engine running, just in case. I stared at him in the rearview mirror and waited for him to draw level with me, but he didn't. Once he was within a hundred yards or so of my car, he stopped in the road.

Jumping from my car in frustration, I clenched my fists and shouted up the road at him, "What do you want from me?"

Again he said nothing, but just sat on his bike,

staring at me from the shadows of his hood.

"Right, you chicken-shit," I said under my breath. "I've had enough of your fun and games." Climbing back into my car, I spun it around in the road and raced towards him. On seeing me coming, he took something white from his coat pocket, leant over on his bike and attached whatever it was onto a branch protruding from the hedgerow. Then swooping left on his bike, he cycled away and sped down a narrow lane set between two fields.

Pulling alongside the lane, I could see it was far too narrow for me to drive my car down. Thumping the steering wheel with my fist, I screamed in anger as I watched him disappear into the distance. Looking to my right, I tried to see what it was he had placed in the bushes. Climbing from my car, I went over to find that the male had skewered a folded piece of paper onto a branch. With the edges of the paper flapping in the breeze, I pulled it free. Unfolding the note, I read what was written upon it.

Sorry, didn't mean to hurt you yesterday. There is more danger to come – be careful.

I looked at the piece of paper and I knew the cyclist had been aware of my presence in the graveyard the whole time. The piece of paper had been torn from a bigger piece. In the far corner, I could just make out the word 'Mary's', which suggested he had taken it from a piece of headed note paper from St. Mary's

103

church. The only opportunity he would've had to write the message was while he'd gone to the church to collect his bike after leaving the graveyard. And if he'd written the note then, he must have been aware of my presence in the graveyard. He then hid somewhere along the road and waited for me to pass him in my car.

Whoever he was, I was certain he meant me no real harm. He'd had a couple of opportunities to do so. But who was he? And why did he have to behave as if he were some kind of guardian angel?

Tucking the note into my jeans pocket, I got back into my car and headed back towards the Inn. As I pulled-up out front, the first specks of snow flurried past on the wind. Hurrying to my room, I pulled the bedcovers over my head and tried to get some rest before my next *vampire shift* began later that evening.

Chapter Ten

I arrived at the police station just before seven. While I'd slept the rest of the day away, it had continued to snow and was now coming down in thick flurries. The narrow streets of The Ragged Cove were covered with it, as were the fields that stretched out on either side of the country roads I'd taken to get to work. Several times, the back wheels of my car had slipped and skidded and I'd had to be careful not to drive head-first into some ditch. So it was with some relief that I arrived at the station without wrecking my second car in less than twenty-four hours.

Hurrying into the station and out of the snow, I found Sergeant Murphy, Potter, and Luke all sitting at their desks behind the front counter. It was as if they were waiting for me. Coming around the front counter, I glanced at Luke and he held my gaze with his brilliant green eyes. The last time I'd seen him, we had been curled up together on my bed in my poky room. I wondered how he felt about that. Luke half-smiled and I looked away. Sometimes I found it hard to look at him, I could sense something between us, but I didn't quite know what. If I were to be honest with myself, I knew that I found his rugged looks attractive, but there was something else – something that told me I should try and keep my distance.

"How are you feeling tonight, constable?"

Sergeant Murphy asked, and I noticed straight away that he hadn't called me by my first name like he had before.

"A bit bruised and battered," I said, placing my uniform and utility belt on the desk in front of me.

"Not as battered as the police car you wrecked last night," Potter chipped in, lighting a cigarette.

I looked across at Luke and he was still staring at me. Ignoring Potter's remark, I turned to face Sergeant Murphy and said, "I don't know if Luke has already briefed you, but there was an incident last night up at the graveyard."

Popping his pipe into his mouth, Murphy looked straight at me and said, "I'd like to hear your account of what took place last night."

"It's difficult to explain without sounding -" I started.

"Without sounding like what?" Potter cut in.

"Like I've lost my mind," I said.

"Tell them what happened," Luke told me. "You're amongst friends here."

Hearing this, I glanced at Potter and wasn't so sure. Turning away from him, I looked at my sergeant and explained how I'd carried out an examination of the open grave.

"When I was down in the hole, I lifted up a piece of the coffin lid to find scratch marks on the underside of it," I told him.

"So?" Potter said, putting out his cigarette and immediately lighting another.

"So," I continued, "it suggested to me only one explanation – and I know this sounds far-fetched – but the girl Kristy Hall must have been buried alive."

"*Buried alive!*" Potter scoffed, squirting streams of blue smoke through his nostrils.

Raising his hand as if to silence Potter, Murphy said, "Let's hear Constable Hudson out before we comment." Then looking at me, he nodded, as if telling me to carry on.

"I also found claw marks on the inside of the grave, again supporting the theory that someone had climbed out rather than in," I told them. "I tried to call Luke on my radio, but it seemed that he either didn't receive my transmission or there wasn't any signal. I climbed out of the grave to find Kristy Hall standing there."

"Oh this is just such a lot of old bollocks," Potter cut in again.

"Be quiet, Sean!" Murphy snapped, and he sounded as if he were getting angry. "Carry on, constable."

"She looked pale, as if she were sick," I said. "Not only that, she was covered in earth and mud. She kept asking for her mother. I asked her if I could help her, but she kept saying she was hungry." I stopped and again I looked at Luke, who was staring at me, his eyes keen and sharp-looking. I couldn't tell if he believed me or not. I wanted to go on with my story, but it was so bizarre I feared I risked my professional reputation before I'd even fully started on my career. I'd been in

107

bother at training school several times and this wasn't going to help. But just like the trouble I'd often found myself in at training school, none of this was my fault.

"Go on," Murphy said, sounding impatient.

Swallowing hard, I said, "Then she started to change."

"Change?" Potter laughed. "What's that supposed to mean?'"

"I won't tell you again, Potter," Murphy hissed. "Put a sock in it, or get out."

Lighting another cigarette, Potter folded his arms across his chest and grinned at me.

Trying to ignore him, I carried on. "The girl began to wail as if in pain. Then I heard this awful sound, like flesh ripping. Her teeth looked as if they had grown." Then closing my eyes, so I didn't have to look at any of them, I added, "The girl had fangs."

I heard a snigger come from the corner of the room and I didn't have to open my eyes to know it was Potter who was laughing at me.

"What happened next?" Sergeant Murphy asked.

"I ran for my life, Sarge," I said, opening my eyes and staring straight into his. "I didn't know what else to do. I kept calling for Luke over the radio, asking for help, but again, I don't think my messages were getting through. I managed to get to the police car, but the creature – or whatever it was – came after me. It smashed the windscreen with its face. I drove the car forward and the *thing* crashed into the graveyard wall. I drove the car at her, but..." I paused.

"But what?" Murphy persisted.

"She escaped," I said as Potter stifled another fit of the giggles. "She leapt away at an incredible speed. I managed to turn the car as I tried to escape. I was injured and my nose was bleeding. As I drove away from the church, the vampire-thing attacked again. She was so fast and strong. She punched her fists through the bonnet as if it were made out of paper."

"If she were so strong and powerful, how did you manage to survive?" Potter smirked.

"I had a crucifix on me, and as she tried to bite me, I stuck it into her mouth. It was almost as if she had swallowed poison. She started to convulse on the bonnet of the car. Her mouth started to foam up and the foam ate through the car's paintwork like acid. Then, before I knew what was happening, she exploded into a pile of ash and dust. Realising that the threat was over, I started to lose consciousness, and before I blacked out, I saw Luke peering in at me through the broken car window," I finished.

"And?" Sergeant Murphy asked me.

"That's all, Sarge." Then glancing quickly at Luke, I added, "The next thing I was aware of was waking in my room this morning."

Without saying a word, Sergeant Murphy sucked on the end of his pipe, not taking his eyes off me. After what seemed like an eternity, Murphy said, "So that is your statement, Constable Hudson?"

"Yes, Sergeant," I said, knowing that I had only

told him what I believed to be the truth.

"You don't wish to change anything?" he asked.

"No, Sergeant."

Standing up, again he was wearing jeans and slippers; he came towards me, his right pelvis sloping to the right as if in need of a hip replacement. "I'd heard good things about you, Hudson," he said, and he sounded almost sad. "Excellent things, in fact. I was led to believe that although you could be a pain in the arse at times, you were however, the most gifted recruit at training school. That's why you were recommended for this difficult posting. I thought you would be an asset to this station – that you would be able to assist us in tracking down those responsible for the killings in The Ragged Cove."

"But that's -"I started, but he spoke over me.

"Instead, I've been sent nothing more than an immature fantasist – a know-it-all," he barked.

"But -"

"In less than twenty-four hours, you've clambered over two crime scenes, destroyed evidence, recklessly destroyed police property – namely one of our only two police vehicles - and have now brought into question your own honesty and integrity by coming up with a pack of lies to excuse your unruly behaviour," he said.

I couldn't believe what I was hearing. I'd done nothing wrong. Every word of my statement had been true. Not prepared to stand by and have my integrity questioned, I spoke up and said, "Have you actually been up to the grave and examined it yourself?" I asked him.

"No, I sent our forensically-trained officer up there today to carry out a proper examination," Murphy said, and looked at Potter.

"What, him?" I asked, and now it was my turn to scoff.

"Yes me!" Potter said. "Got a problem with that, Columbo?"

"Well, if you'd examined it properly, you would've seen what I had," I said.

"Sure - I found the coffin lid – what was left of it after you'd trampled all over it," he sniped.

"And the scratch marks?" I asked.

"There were scratch marks, but they'd been made by animals – foxes, rats, badgers – after the girl's body had been removed," he said

I couldn't believe what I was hearing. "Are you being serious?" I said. "What about footprints?"

"Well to be honest, after you had stomped all over it in your boots, it was hard to see anything. But after a careful and *thorough* examination, the only footprints I could find were yours and Luke's. So if this *vampire-girl* had chased you across the graveyard, I found no footprints – only yours," he smiled at me.

"What about the damage to the car?" I asked him.

"What about it?"

"The broken windscreen?"

"By the state of your face tonight, it looks like

you're the one who smashed through it," he said. "As for the scratches across the bonnet and sides of the car, it is my opinion that they were caused by your reckless driving as you scraped against the stone walls up at the church and the branches and thorns from the overgrown hedgerows."

"What about the acid burns?" I asked.

"You've already admitted to driving the car straight into the wall up at the graveyard, and in doing so, you crushed the battery which ruptured and sprayed the bonnet with battery acid," he smiled.

"I don't believe this," I groaned.

"No, we don't believe *you*," Sergeant Murphy said.

Turning to Luke I said, "You were up there. You must have seen something?"

Looking at me, his eyes almost grey, Luke slowly shook his head and said, "I'm sorry, Kiera, but all I saw was you driving away at a high speed from the church and crashing the car."

"So you didn't see the girl?" I asked, almost pleading with him.

"Sorry, Kiera, I didn't see any girl," he said. "As soon as I saw you racing away in the police car, I came running after you."

I glanced down at his trousers and knew that he was lying. Knowing that whatever I said wouldn't be believed, I looked at Sergeant Murphy. "So what happens now?"

"You go back to headquarters," he said. "I don't

have room for a liar in my station."

"But…" I began.

"Don't worry about your precious record, I'll tell them that you were homesick – the climate down here didn't agree with you. I won't drop you in the shit with Sergeant Phillips. I'm not that kind of bloke."

Hearing this made my blood boil, and I could feel tears standing in my eyes. They had no right to treat me like this. Clenching my fists by my side, I took a deep breath and then let loose. "You make me laugh. You couldn't solve a game of Cluedo, let alone a series of brutal killings," I seethed. "For the last few years, you've had people go missing, graves desecrated, over twenty brutal murders, a string of police officers have disappeared off the face of the Earth, and you have the nerve to stand there and tell me I'm no good at my job!"

"Hang on a minute!" Potter said coming forward.

"Let her say her piece," Murphy said. "Because when she's finished, she's out of here."

"You accuse me of destroying crime scenes, when you let that cretin stand and smoke over the mutilated body of an eight-year-old child. And as for you," I said, looking Murphy up and down, "you're the most unprofessional sergeant I've ever come across. You're meant to be representing the police service and you lounge around the office in jeans and slippers, with a pipe hanging from your mouth. And as for calling Force Headquarters – go on – I dare you. Or perhaps you haven't noticed that none of the telephones work in this godforsaken place. Nothing works! The shops hardly ever open, the streets are pretty much deserted and you can only speak with a police officer at night. Now I don't know about you – but this place seems fucked-up!"

"What's the point in being on duty during the day when most of the crime in this town happens at night?" Potter cut in. "That's just good police work."

"Good police work!" I laughed at him. "I haven't actually seen you *do* any police work since I arrived. If your idea of good police work is smoking yourself to death in this office, then you're very good at it."

Then pausing to draw breath, someone cut in and said, "Have you finished, constable?"

Spinning around to see who had spoken, I was shocked to find a tall, lean-looking man standing in the corner by the passageway that led to the cells. He hadn't come in via the front entrance and I knew from the tour Potter had given me the night before that there was no other way into the station.

The man was about six-foot-four, with steely-white hair that was combed back off his narrow forehead. He looked as if he were in his late fifties but was in good shape. I could tell by his tanned, dry skin he had recently come back from his holidays, which had been spent in a hot climate. He had strong, muscular hands. His thumbs were looped through his belt loops. He wore a police uniform, and by the three silver pips on each shoulder, I knew he was a chief inspector.

"I said, have you finished, constable?" he asked me again, and his bright blue eyes bored straight into mine.

"Yes, sir," I said.

"Then let me introduce myself. I am Chief Inspector Rom. And this station and its officers are under my charge," he said in a low, grim-sounding voice. "If you feel you have a complaint on how my officers perform then feel free to raise your concerns with me." Then coming forward, his eyes never leaving mine, he stood before me and whispered, "But one thing I do know, is that I don't need some snotty-nosed recruit coming into my kingdom and telling me how to run things. Do you understand?"

Looking up at him, I said, "Yes sir, I understand."

"Now if you would be so kind as to gather up your uniform, leave this station, and don't ever come back," he said. "Tomorrow morning you are to travel back to force headquarters where you will be assigned a new posting. And believe me when I tell you that the report I will be sending about you, won't be as charitable as Sergeant Murphy's. Now get out of my sight."

Feeling as if I'd been kicked in the guts, I picked up my jacket and made my way around the front desk and left the station. As I went, I couldn't help but notice they were all staring at me, Luke included. Stepping out into the cold, flakes of snow stung my face and covered my hair and shoulders. Climbing into my car and slamming the door shut, the tears I'd been fighting back in the office now ran down my cheeks in warm streams. Jumping, I looked up as someone appeared at the window. Luke stood beside my car, his black hair now looking white with snow. He knocked on the glass.

"Kiera!" he shouted.

Wiping away my tears with the back of my hand as I didn't want him to see me crying, I opened the window an inch and said through the gap, "What do you want?"

"What are you going to do?" he asked.

"I'm going home," I told him.

"I'll come up to the Inn and see you before you go," he said.

"Don't bother. I won't be there."

"What's that supposed to mean?"

"I'm going *home* now," I told him. Then looking through the gap in the window at him, I said, "You know what, Luke? I thought we were friends. I thought we had a connection. I mean, you stayed with me last night."

"I am your friend," he said, brushing snow out of his eyes so he could see me.

"It didn't seem like that in there!" I snapped.

"What could I say?" he said.

"You could've told the truth."

"I did!"

"You're a liar, Luke Bishop," I said, looking straight into his green eyes. Then winding up the window, I said, "Goodbye."

Without looking back at him standing in the

oncoming blizzard, I pressed my foot down hard on the accelerator and headed out of The Ragged Cove.

Chapter Eleven

The engine of my little car groaned as I forced it up the narrow, snow-covered roads and away from the town below. Fierce gusts of wind shook its very frame and the wipers worked overtime to clear the snow.

I'd cranked the heater up to full blast, but it did nothing to take away the freezing chill. Even inside the car, wispy plumes of breath escaped from my mouth and nose and covered the windscreen in a misty film, making visibility almost zero. Leaning forward, I peered out, desperate not to steer off the road and into some ditch. I knew that if I could just reach a main road, the chances were that it would have been gritted with salt and I would be able to make my way home to Havensfield without incident. Even if I had to drive all night, I was determined to get there. I hadn't even stopped at the Crescent Moon Inn to collect my stuff – I would pay to have it forwarded to me at a later date.

I just wanted to be away from The Ragged Cove; but more than that, I wanted to be as far away from Luke as possible. I didn't care if I ever saw him again. I felt crushed inside at how he had treated me back at the station and how he'd lied about what had taken place up at the graveyard. I knew he had seen that girl – *I knew it!* If only my friend Tom had been posted to the Ragged Cove too, we would have solved the mystery of this place in a blink of an eye. He would have believed me and he definitely wouldn't have lied. Tom knew that being a cop stood for something. Christ, even my colleague constable John Miles, who wasn't the brightest of sparks, would've seen that The Ragged Cove was seriously messed up. So, why wouldn't Sergeant Murphy and his team *see* it too? Deep down, I knew they did, but for whatever reason they pretended not to.

Wiping at the inside of the windscreen with the back of my hand, I could just make out a sign fixed to the side of the road. As my car crawled towards it, my heart almost leapt with joy. The sign read:

You are leaving The Ragged Cove
Please drive carefully!

Feeling as if I were returning to civilisation – *the real world* – where mobile phones worked, radios got a signal, shops stayed open, and vampires didn't chase you around graveyards in the middle of the night, I almost felt like punching the air with joy. Taking one hand from the wheel, I switched on the radio and my heart sank as the sound of static hissed through the speakers.

But then, as my car inched towards the sign, I heard something faint – a sound within the static and it sounded like music. Turning the dial on the radio, I leant forward and to my joy, I could hear the sweet voice of Adele singing 'Someone like you'.

"C'mon," I said aloud. "I want to hear you!"

Her voice was faint, almost like she was lost somewhere within the static, but with every inch my car took towards that sign, her voice became clearer. Turning the dial in the hope of picking up a clearer signal, I took my eyes off the road for what seemed just like a second. But in that moment, I hadn't seen the sheet of black ice covering the road. The back end of my car skidded right, then left as I gripped the wheel and screamed, "No!"

The Mini spun out of my control and headed for a huge drift of snow. Thumping into the ancient stone wall that lined the road, the car tilted right, and for a moment I thought it was going to tip over onto its side. Slamming my hands against the dashboard to steady myself, the car nose-dived into a ditch, its rear wheels lifting off the road. Leaning forward in my seat, my chest pressed against the steering wheel, the voice of Adele began to fade until the sound of static seemed almost deafening.

Pushing against the car door, I clambered free of the car and fell into the snow outside. At once, my nose, ears, and hands began to sting with the cold. Shielding my eyes against the blizzard, I looked around, trying to get some bearings. The sign telling me I was so close to escaping The Ragged Cove was behind me and it seemed to taunt me. Turning my back to it, I peered back in the direction I had come, and some miles in the distance, I could just make out the twinkling lights of the town. Looming up into the night like a twisted finger, I could see the steeple of the church in the dark.

Cupping my hands around my mouth, I blew into them. They were fast going numb. Turning to look at my car sticking up out of the ditch, I leant against the boot and tried to force the rear wheels back onto the road.

"Please!" I groaned. "I just wanna get out of this godforsaken place. Is that too much to ask?" I shouted into the dark.

The car rocked up and down like a seesaw, but however much I tried, I couldn't get the car out of the ditch. With each passing minute, the snow grew deeper and deeper around my shins.

Knowing I had to make a decision as to what I was going to do, I considered my options. I could stay in the car and hope that someone came by and helped me, but the chances of anyone being out on a night like this was remote. The roads were fast becoming impassable, so I knew there was little chance of being rescued by a passer-by. I could stay in the car with the heaters running, but I doubted they could melt an ice cube, and I would more than likely freeze to death. I didn't have any blankets or warm clothing in the boot, and the rate the snow was coming down, my little car would be covered within a couple of hours. I didn't fancy dying entombed in a 1960's Mini, buried beneath a mountain of snow.

Remembering my mobile phone, I rummaged for it in my pocket. Pulling it out, I looked at the signal bar which continued to glow red. Holding the phone above my head, I tried to search for a signal.

"Please!" I hissed. "Just give me a break. I

deserve one with everything that I've been through!"

But however much I turned and moved towards the border, the signal bar remained that constant, angry red. Putting the phone away, I looked back at the town below me. I figured that if I crossed the fields, it could be no more than a couple of miles away. I could stick to the road, but it wasn't as direct with all its twists and turns and would probably double the distance of my journey. But however much my life depended on it, I really didn't want to go back there. What was I going back to and how many days would I have to spend there before the snow eased and I could get my car back onto the road? I really didn't want to go back to that Inn, and now that I'd been banned from the police station, I had no reason to be there. I didn't know if I could face any of them again – I didn't know if I could face *Luke* again. But I couldn't stay out on the road. Not only was I exposed to the freezing weather, I was a sitting target for vampires.

So taking my torch from the car, I pulled the collar of my jacket up and set off across the fields, back towards The Ragged Cove.

Bent forward at the waist to protect myself from the freezing wind and falling snow, I trudged across the fields. The snow was falling so hard and fast that when I glanced back at my car in the distance, I could hardly see its little red frame and my tracks had already been covered. Ahead and to the right, I could see what looked like a wooded area. So cutting diagonally across the field, I made my way towards it, hoping that the trees would offer me some shelter.

The snow whipped and howled all around me, and in the noise of the wind, I was sure that I could hear the far off sound of screaming. Looking in the direction of those cries, I thought I saw shadows flitting back and forth across the skyline. Turning around in the snow, trying to locate those sounds was disorientating and it wasn't long before I had lost all sense of direction. Peering into the distance, I was sure I could see a dark smudge on the horizon, and hoping that it was the wooded area, I set off towards it.

I hadn't gone far when I noticed the dark smudge had changed and now looked like three dark shapes in the distance.

"What's that?" I said, shielding my eyes with my hands, trying to work out what the shapes were. With every second they seemed to get closer and they were coming straight towards me. As they got closer still, I thought that perhaps they were three people, but that couldn't be right. They were travelling way too fast. No one could move with such speed and agility in the heavy snow.

With my heart almost stopping, I realised the shapes coming towards me *were* people, and they weren't walking, they were *running* towards me at an incredible speed, as if they were soaring just inches above the snow. Realising I was in incredible danger, I ran as fast as I could, hoping I was heading towards the shelter of the trees.

My progress was slow, hampered by the

deepness of the snow, which was now level with my knees. Looking back, the three figures were now so close I could hear the sound of the rushing wind their speed created, whipping up the snow beneath them and spraying it into the night.

"No! Please God, no!" I cried, staggering forward and losing my footing. Panicked, I clawed myself back onto my feet. My whole body trembled – not because of the cold – but in fear. My legs felt as if they were going to give way at any moment and I desperately needed to pee. Not sure which direction I was headed, I stumbled on, tears running down my face through sheer terror.

Sucking in mouthfuls of freezing cold air to try and calm myself, I turned around to see the three vampires racing towards me, their gleaming white teeth glistening like razors in the night. Standing rooted to the spot, I screamed. Within touching distance of me, one of them darted left and the other right, so as to surround me.

"Stay away from me!" I screamed.

They circled, zipping back and forth as if examining their prey. The third one raced forward, its eyes burning red and mouth drooling. Shrieking, it grabbed for me, its claws skimming just inches from my face. I ducked, dropping into the snow. Glancing up, I watched as it raced away. My heart almost stopped. The vampire was wearing what appeared to be a ripped and dishevelled-looking police uniform. Without having time to comprehend what I'd seen, the vampire leapt into the air, corkscrewed around, landed and raced back towards me. It was like it raced over the surface of the snow instead of sinking into it.

Knowing I had nowhere to run or hide, I covered my face with my hands and prayed my death would be quick. With the sound of its screaming coming out of the dark at me, I closed my eyes and waited to be taken. Then there was another sound, almost deafening. It was like the loudest thunderclap I'd ever heard.

"What was that?" I shouted in shock, snapping open my eyes. I caught a fleeting glimpse of a winged creature soar across my eye line, snatching away the vampire who was just about to take hold of me.

Pulling myself out of the snow, I looked up to see what it was. But it moved with such speed and agility, it looked like nothing more than a fluttering blur of shadows. The vampire in the police uniform was yanked this way and that in the sky just above my head.

It tried to fight back against whatever it was that had hold of it. Shielding my eyes against the snow, I could see that whatever it was appeared to be stripped to the waist. The creature's skin was as pale as the snow that fell all around it. Its hair was black, just like the wings that protruded from its back. But it moved too fast for me to really see it. Not knowing if this creature were my saviour or if it had its own plans for me, I turned and fled.

With my heart racing like a trip hammer, I stumbled, got up, stumbled again, until I was near exhaustion. Looking back over my shoulder, not wanting to lose sight of the other two vampires, I saw the one in the police uniform arch its back and throw its arms wide as it became consumed by the creature in the sky. With an ear-splitting scream, one of the other vampires chased after me.

"Get away!" I screeched, stumbling backwards into the snow, landing on my arse and knocking the wind from me. Covering my ears with my hands, I looked past the approaching vampire and saw the shadowy creature rip out the throat of the vampire in the police uniform. Blood sprayed into the night and spattered the snow around me in crimson streaks. Then my rescuer – *if that's what it was* – soared away in a fluttering blur, tossing the second vampire, who was almost upon me, through the air like a rag doll. This one was female and from where I lay in the snow, I could see she was wearing a floral-patterned dress. Her bright auburn hair fanned out in the wind.

To the right of me, I heard the gut-wrenching sound of screaming as the third and final vampire took their chance and raced towards me. Turning, I tried to run away, but the creature was too quick. And by the time I'd felt its hot breath against my neck, it had snatched hold of me with its talon-like hands and leapt into a nearby tree.

Kicking out frantically, my stomach lurched as I watched the ground disappear beneath my feet at an incredible speed, as the vampire scrambled up the trunk of the tree with me clutched in its arms. Within seconds, I was looking down at the tops of the trees. Looking left and right, I could see that the vampire had its claws hooked into my jacket.

"Get the fuck off me!" I roared. "Put me down!"

Glancing up into its face, it looked white and contorted as if in constant pain. Just like the others, its eyes burned red as if its brain was on fire in its misshapen skull. The vampire's forehead was pronounced and its brow appeared to almost hang over its eyes like a ledge. Its nose looked more like a snout and its mouth was like an open wound, fleshy lips pulled back, revealing a bloody set of gums, crammed full of razor-sharp teeth.

Dragging me higher into the tree, I screamed. Ahead, I could see the flutter of white and black as the flying creature tore the female vampire in two, casting the remains of her body in opposite directions.

"Let me go!" I screamed, kicking and struggling wildly.

Hearing my screams, the winged creature flew towards us and again, the night was torn open by the sound of that thunderclap. Within an instance, it was upon us, its form shimmering so much as to make it impossible to truly see who or *what* it was.

As the shadowy form attacked the vampire who had hold of me, its claws dug deeper into my jacket and flesh. The pain was excruciating. Reaching into my pocket, my fingers brushed against the small bottle of holy water given to me at breakfast by the old woman. Crying out in pain, I unscrewed the cap. Reaching round,

I poured some of the water onto the vampire's claws. Almost at once its flesh began to bubble and blister. Tendrils of smoke started to rise from its white flesh.

Shrieking in agony, the vampire let go of me and I tumbled out of the tree and towards the ground. Over the sound of the wind whistling in my ears, I heard the vampire howl one last time as the winged creature tore it apart.

"Help me!" I cried looking down as the snow-covered fields raced towards me. Closing my eyes, and for the second time that night hoping my death would be quick and painless, I felt myself soaring upwards and away from the ground.

Opening one eye, I peered out and could see I was in the arms of the creature that had saved me from the vampires. My face was pressed against his naked chest, which felt as cold as the night air that rushed past me. Glancing up to get a peek at its face, whatever it was, arched its wings so that it fell into shadow, masking its identity.

"Hold tight." Its voice was a deep growl.

Locked in the creature's muscular arms, we raced through the night and back towards The Ragged Cove. I looked down and could see the snow covered fields and treetops whizzing past in a near blur. Glancing right, desperate to see the face of the creature, I saw that its wings were tattered-looking and worn. They rippled in the freezing night air that rushed over us. He flew through the night at such speed, my hair whipped about my face. Out of sheer instinct to survive, I gripped the creature's hands that held my waist. But they weren't hands – not really. They were long strong claws. Each finger was pointed like a blade.

"Where are you taking me?" I asked over the roar of the wind.

But instead of answering my question, the winged creature suddenly plummeted out of the sky with such speed that my stomach lurched. I began to feel dizzy. That ear-shattering thunderclap came again and everything went black.

Chapter Twelve

Opening my eyes, it took a moment for me to realise I was lying on the bed back in my room at the Crescent Moon Inn. The lamp on the desk had been switched on and my room was bathed in a warm, orange glow. I didn't know how long I'd been unconscious, and my shoulders felt raw. Touching them, I remembered the vampire digging his claws into me. I remembered being rescued by that winged creature and I sat up. It was then I noticed someone sitting in the shadows in the corner of the room.

"Who's there?" I asked, and my throat felt sore from all the screaming I'd done earlier that night.

"It's just me," the figure said, standing up and moving into the light.

Watching Luke step from the shadows, I groaned, "What do you want?" I still felt angry towards him for what had happened at the police station.

"I just popped by to see if you were okay," he said, coming closer.

Laying back down and turning away from him, I said, "Well, now that you can see I'm fine, you can go. I have nothing to say to you."

"I thought you were leaving town?" he said.

"It didn't quite work out that way," I said, my back still facing him. "Anyway, how did you know I was here?"

"I drove past and saw the lamp on in your room, so I thought..." he started.

Rolling over to face him, I said, "How did you get in here?"

"Your door was open," he told me.

"Well if you don't mind," I said, "you can go now and close the door behind you."

"What's wrong with you?" he asked, looking down at me.

"What's wrong with *me*?" I hissed, sitting up on my bed. "You lied back there at the station. You could've got me out of trouble."

"How?"

"You said you didn't see anything," I started. "You claimed that you only saw me drive away in the police car, and then you came running after me once I'd crashed the car."

"That's right," he said, trying to hold my stare.

"You didn't run anywhere that night," I told him. "You must have been right on top of me when that car crashed, which means you must have seen that vampire."

Luke shook his head in denial.

"It was raining that night, Luke," I reminded him. "There were mud and puddles everywhere. If you'd ran down that road like you claimed to have done, then the bottoms of your trousers would've been splashed with mud." Looking down at the hems of his trousers, I added, "See, there's not a fleck of mud on them."

"These are a different pair of trousers," he said.

"Liar," I snapped. "They're the trousers you had on last night up at the graveyard."

"How do you know that?" he asked me.

Pointing to his right thigh, I said, "Egg and ketchup, that's how I know!"

"What?" he asked, sounding baffled.

"Last night in the police car, I said I knew you had an egg sandwich for your dinner because you had dripped egg and ketchup down the front of your tie and trousers," I reminded him. "The stains are still there, Luke, but I can't see any mud."

Glancing down at the stain, then back at me, he said "You don't miss a trick, do you, Kiera?"

Thinking for a moment, I said, "Perhaps I do."

"What do you mean?"

"Well, if you didn't run down that lane, how did you get to me and the car so quickly?" I said. "That's what I can't figure out."

Staring at me with his pale green eyes, Luke said, "Kiera, I can't lie to you anymore." Then taking off his jacket, he unbuttoned his shirt and let it flutter to the floor.

Holding up my hand, I said, "I'm flattered, Luke, but I'm not sure if this is such a good idea."

Staring at me with such intensity, it felt as if he were looking into my very soul, he said, "No, Kiera. You don't understand."

"Understand what?" I started, trying hard not to notice his well-defined chest and flat stomach.

"This," he said turning around.

Shrinking back on my bed, I watched as Luke's shoulder blades rippled beneath his pale skin. The tissue and muscles on his back shifted and stretched as what looked like a series of black bones grew from his back. Luke rocked forward as if in pain, the black bones reaching up out of his ribcage and shoulders. A thin, silky membrane hung beneath the bones and I could see that he was growing a pair of wings.

They reminded me of the pterodactyl dinosaurs my father had shown me in picture books as a girl. Each wing seemed to have a long bony shoulder and arm that was about six feet in length. Beneath this arm hung the wing, which was a see-through, stretchy-looking membrane. At the end of each arm protruded a wrist and attached to these were three skeletal fingers.

Covering my mouth with my hands, I watched in disbelief and wonder as Luke shook from head to foot, the metamorphosis complete. His huge, black wings stretched out on either side of him. Turning around, his arms by his sides, Luke looked at me.

"Please don't freak out," he said.

"Whoa," I breathed.

"Is that all you have to say?" he asked me, and it was as he spoke I noticed his two front incisors had grown into two, long sharpened points.

"What do you want me to say?" I whispered in awe. Although I should've been terrified by the creature that stood before me, I wasn't. Luke looked like an angel – a *dark* angel. If it were possible, his eyes glowed greener than before, his skin looked as smooth and as white as marble, and his lips were a dark, blood red. His jet-black hair shone like an onyx stone.

"How long have you been able to do that...that *thing* with the wings, exactly?" I asked.

"Forever," he said. There was a moment's silence, neither of us not knowing what to say next.

"How do I look?" he suddenly asked with a nervous smile, still unsure of what my reaction was going to be at seeing him like this.

"You look stunning," I breathed.

"Stunning?" he smiled. "Shouldn't that be *handsome*?"'

"No, you look more than that," I told him, a warm sensation flowing over me. "It was you?"

"What was?"

"It was you who saved me from those vampires tonight?" I asked.

"Yes, it was."

Curious as to what that made him, I said, "So are you like them? A vampire, I mean?"

Coming towards me, Luke sat on the edge of my bed, and I couldn't help but notice how his wings seemed to tremor as he moved. Looking into my eyes, he said, "Some would call me a vampire, but I'm a Vampyrus."

"A Vampyrus?" I asked, confused.

"The Vampyrus are what humans would commonly call *Desmodus Rotundas*."

"The what?"

"Vampire bats," he said.

Trying to understand what he was telling me, I said, "So where do you live – *hang out*? Where do you come from?"

"I come from The Hollows," he said, and his voice sounded distant as if he were picturing it in his mind. "The Hollows are the caves and the caverns beneath us."

"So you live underground then?" I said, confused. "So like there's a whole race of you living down there?"

"There always has been," he explained. "Even before humans, the Vampyrus have lived in the holes, the tunnels, and the caverns that exist beneath the Earth."

"So why are you masquerading as a police officer up here?" I asked him, and if it wasn't for the fact that I had a winged man sitting at the foot of my bed, I wouldn't have believed a word of what I was being told.

"We've come to hunt out one of our own," he told me, and his eyes had grown dark, their spark faded.

"Why? What has this Vampyrus done?"

"Kiera," he said, "for hundreds of years our race has been travelling up to the surface. Some of us have managed to secretly work our way into the highest levels and positions in your society. But all of us, up until now, have respected your rules, your laws and your world. But there is one who has broken those rules, and instead of returning to The Hollows to satisfy hIs hunger, he's given into his desires and taken human blood. By doing this, he's created a mutant breed, a half-human and half-Vampyrus – they are what your race calls vampires. They are the dead – the *undead*."

"Who is this Vampyrus?" I asked him.

"We don't know," Luke confessed. "But we have managed to track him down to The Ragged Cove. It is somewhere here in which he hides."

"But he can't be that hard to find," I said. "I mean, you must be able to recognise one of your own when you see them."

"But how?" he asked. "Didn't you believe me to be human? Could you tell by looking at me that I wasn't like you?"

Shaking my head, I said, "Well no, I guess."

"Then you can see the challenge that faces us," he said. "But the longer it takes us to find him, the more he will feed and the more vampires will be created – until one day your world will be infested with them."

"Why doesn't he just stop?" I asked. "If he can see the damage he is causing, why doesn't he go back underground until his hunger passes?"

"Once tasted, human blood becomes an unbreakable addiction," he told me. "And that need – *desire* – never goes away. I've heard it described as being like a fire in your soul that can't be put out."

"So he can't be cured of this craving?"

"There have been others throughout history who have come and fed," he said just above a whisper.

"And they were cured?" I asked.

"Yes."

"How?"

"Like me, Vampyrus were sent to hunt them down and destroy them," he told me, his eyes turning dark.

"So you're not like a regular vampire – what I mean is, you can go out in the light?" I asked him.

"Our natural habitat is darkness, but some of us can tolerate daylight," he explained. "As for me, I'm not a great lover of the sun. I can put up with it for a few hours before my skin starts to itch and blister. Others last only minutes before their skin starts to smoke."

"So are you like those other vampires?" I asked him, remembering how he had reacted to my cut wrist and how I'd seen him sniff the blood stains on the sweatshirt. "What I'm trying to ask is – do *you* need blood – *human* blood to survive?"

"It depends," he said.

"On what?" I asked, letting go of his hand.

Sensing my concern, Luke said. "You don't need to be scared of me. Very much like the sun, it's different for each of the Vampyrus. Some of us hunger for human blood as soon as we come above ground, some of us can last hours, days, or weeks without feeling the hunger – but when it comes, we have to go back below until the desire for blood fades. Then we can come back again."

"So what about you?" I asked him. "How long can you last, before your *hunger* becomes too much?"

"About six weeks," he said.

"So how long before you have to go back?"

"About a week," he smiled, "so you're safe for the moment. I felt it the other day when you cut your wrist. The smell of it made me feel crazy for a moment. That's why I didn't want to get too close to you."

"I saw you sniffing the bloodstains that I'd left on your sweatshirt," I confessed.

Looking embarrassed, Luke looked away and said, "I couldn't help myself. The smell of your blood was beautiful – *intoxicating*."

Wanting to know more about him and his life below ground, I asked, "So how do you come above ground – how do you get here?"

"We come up via wells dug by humans, the potholes and drains. Luckily for us, you don't yet have the ability to reach the thousands of miles and network of tunnels and caves beneath your feet. But mostly, we burrow our own way out and protect it with a trapdoor, which we lock, until we're ready to go back. Then we fill it in again."

Sitting quietly for a moment, trying to absorb everything he had told me, I looked at him and said, "Who's *we*?"

"What do you mean?" he asked, looking as if he had slipped up in some way.

"You said, 'We lock it.' Who's *we*?" I asked again.

Looking me straight in the eyes, he smiled, "Murphy, Potter, and Rom."

I couldn't believe what I was hearing. "So you're

telling me that Sergeant Murphy, Chief Inspector Rom, and that dickhead, Potter, are all like you – *vampire bats*?"

Laughing, Luke said, "I know it's hard to believe but they're not really all that bad."

"They seemed pretty bad today," I reminded him.

"Believe it or not, they were just trying to protect you," he told me.

"Protect me!" I scoffed. "They had a funny way of showing it."

"We knew that once you'd killed that vampire last night, they might come after you," he said, and this time he took my hand in his. "We were sending you away from The Ragged Cove for your own safety. We knew we had to get you away from here.'"

"I don't need your protection," I said. "I can look after myself."

"And what about tonight?" he reminded me. "If I hadn't of shown up, you would be dead now - or one of *them*."

Sitting silently for a moment, I looked at him and said, "Well, I'm staying. I can't go back now."

"That's your choice, Kiera. But what lies ahead will be dangerous. Not only for you but for my people as well," he warned me. Then reaching out and brushing a wisp of hair from my face, he said, "You know you don't have to stay, I could get you out of here if you really wanted me to."

Cupping my hand around his, I smiled, "You

need me."

"How do you work that out?"

"Like I said, you, Murphy and Potter couldn't solve a game of Cluedo," I smiled.

Staring at me as if he was about to say something, he suddenly let go of my hand and stood up.

"What were you going to say?" I asked him, a nervous feeling passing through me.

"It doesn't matter," he said, turning his back towards me, his wings making a soft whispering sound.

Standing, I went to him. I wanted to reach out and touch his shoulder, but I didn't know if I should. To do so, meant I would have to touch his wings.

"It does matter," I said.

Turning around, Luke moved closer, his naked chest inches from me. "I was wondering if there was another reason why you might want to stay?"

Knowing exactly what he meant, I lied, "I don't know what you mean," and leant in towards him.

"I was hoping..." he said, but didn't finish.

"Hoping what?" I pushed.

"You're trembling," he smiled, bringing his face closer to mine.

"Am I?"

"Are you afraid?" he whispered, his lips hovering over mine.

"No," I smiled. "But you should be."

"And why's that?" he asked.

"Because I've got a bottle of holy water and a crucifix in my pocket," I whispered.

"They only work on vampires, I'm a *bat*," he smiled, then taking me in his wings, he kissed me.

For such a fierce creature, his kiss was soft as his lips pressed over mine. I closed my eyes as he held me close. But in the darkness, all I could see was Luke tearing those vampires to shreds with his razor-like claws. I saw the jets of blood turning the white snow crimson. I had only been kissed by one man before and he had been human at least. And although Luke's kiss was tender and made my skin tingle and heart race, he wasn't like...

"I'm sorry," I said, easing myself from his arms.

"No, it's me who should be sorry," Luke said. "I shouldn't have kissed you."

"No, it's not that..." I said, struggling to find the right words. I broke his gaze, looking away. His stare could be so intense sometimes.

"Is there someone else...another...?" Luke started.

"No, not really," I tried to explain, those feelings I'd once had for my friend, Tom, threatening to break my heart again. "His name was Tom, but he's gone now."

"What happened?" Luke asked, his voice soft – comforting.

"I promised I would never say," I said. Then, looking back at him, I added. "What about you? Is there no one..."

"There was...once...a long time ago now," he said, wings almost seeming to hum about his broad shoulders. "But I try to forget."

"Does that help?" I asked him, knowing deep in my heart that I would never be able to love another unless I forgot what I had once shared with Tom.

"I could help you to forget," Luke whispered, taking me in his arms again.

"How?" I asked, looking up into his eyes.

He answered my question by kissing me again.

Chapter Thirteen

Luke left me just before dawn. As I had been wrapped in his wings, I'd asked him where he lived. He explained that he slept during the day, along with the other Vampyrus – Murphy and Potter – in the cells at the station. He told me it was close to their hatch, should they need to go back beneath ground in a hurry. When I asked about Chief Inspector Rom, he said that Rom spent most of his time below ground, but didn't explain why.

I'd asked where this *hatch* to The Hollows was and Luke reminded me of the padlocked grate in the corridor that led to the small cellblock back at the station. I was surprised by this – not about its location – but by its ordinariness. It was nondescript, black metal, with a big rusty looking padlock. Leaving me feeling sleepy and the most at peace I'd felt since arriving in The Ragged Cove, Luke told me to meet him at the police station at seven that night.

"But I thought I was banned?" I said, feeling half asleep.

"I'll speak to the others," he assured me.

Then taking my face in his hands, he kissed me. His lips were full and soft, and they lingered over mine. Kissing him back, I could feel his fangs, but in a strange way it didn't seem unnatural. When he kissed me, the feelings I felt were so intense, they almost consumed me. It was as if he had cast me under some kind of spell. With his soft wings around me, I felt protected – *safe*. Enclosed in them, my skin against his, I felt as if everything outside of them didn't exist. It was that moment that mattered – nothing else. My feelings for him felt very sudden and intense and I had no real understanding as to why. All I knew was that these new emotions were in some way intoxicating.

Not wanting him to leave me, I clung to him. "Stay," I whispered.

Brushing his lips over mine, he said, "I can't, Kiera, I need to get back."

Releasing him from my grasp, I watched as he rolled back his shoulders and his wings disappeared back between his shoulder blades. Putting his police shirt back on and buttoning it up the front, it seemed hard to believe what he kept hidden beneath it. Back in his uniform, he looked like any regular cop. He headed towards the door. Luke opened it an inch, then stopped and looked back at me.

"How do you feel about your friend Tom, now?" he asked.

"Tom?" I frowned. "Who's Tom?"

"The guy you told me about – the one you once loved," Luke said.

"I've never been in love before," I frowned. I had no idea as to what he was talking about. "I've never had a friend called Tom."

"It must be my mistake," he half smiled at me. "See you tonight, beautiful girl," Luke added, and then he was gone, closing the door behind him.

Rolling onto my back and pulling the covers over me, I drifted into sleep imagining those soft and powerful wings all around me, brushing against my skin and making me feel safe.

I found myself running along the shore of the cove. I was out of breath. The sea crashed against the sand in thick, black, oily waves. Smashing against the rocks, giant sheets of freezing cold water sprayed into the night. Ahead, there were two huge cliffs stretching up into the sky like deformed monsters. Behind me there was a noise and it sounded like a frantic heartbeat. Gasping for breath, I could see a cloud. It was dark and moved across the night sky at a great speed. The sound of the racing heartbeat came from it.

Turning, I ran hard, clambering over the rocks that jutted from the sand like broken gravestones. Seaweed covered them like black veins. I lost my footing and slipped, falling face-first into the sand. Waves rushed at me, soaking my clothes, face and hair. The heartbeat sound grew louder. Looking back over my shoulder, I could see the cloud was getting nearer, as if it were following me.

Dragging myself to my feet, I ran on, a stitch burning in my side like a stab wound. Giant waves rushed me again, as if wanting to drag me under. Reaching a huge, slick-looking rock, I climbed on top. Looking into the distance, I could see a cave set between the two cliffs ahead of me.

The sound of the heartbeat was louder, almost deafening now. Glancing back again, I screamed. The cloud was almost above me, and I could now see that it wasn't a cloud at all, but a thousand winged creatures racing towards me. The heartbeat was the sound of their wings beating together as one.

Scrambling down the other side of the rock, I raced as fast and as hard as I could towards the cave. Sand kicked up from beneath my trainers, and my jeans felt heavy and wet against my legs, making any movements sluggish. I pushed on, my lungs burning inside me. Looking back, I could see thousands of vampire bats swooping out of the sky. But they weren't normal vampire bats —they were men and women with black wings that looked as if they were made of stretched leather. They were so close I could see their green eyes and the saliva dripping from their razor-sharp teeth.

Turning my back on the Vampyrus, I rushed towards the mouth of the cave. My heart felt like it was going to explode, but I pushed myself harder, faster! The safety of the cave was within touching distance, but as I reached it, I could see it had been sealed over with a metal grate. I yanked on it, but it was locked fast and wouldn't open.

"Please!" I begged. "Please let me in!"

Peering over my shoulder, eyes bulging in fear, I could see the Vampyrus racing towards me, soaring just inches above the sand. Turning to face the grate, I pulled on it with what little strength I had left.

"Please open!" I screamed.

Sand and seawater sprayed up all around me under the force of the beating wings of the vampire bats that were now within touching distance of me. Pulling on the grate one last time, it opened and I stumbled through it and into the waiting arms of my...

"...mum!" I yelled, bolting upright in my bed. My heart was racing in my chest, and I felt breathless. A thin layer of sweat covered my brow and my black hair clung to my face in damp streaks. Throwing back the covers, I swung my legs over the side of the bed and stood up. They felt shaky and unstable. Going to the bathroom, I poured myself a glass of water from the tap and drank it down without stopping until the glass was empty.

The dream about my mother had upset me, and as I looked in the mirror above the bathroom sink, I brushed away the tears that were rolling down my cheeks. I hadn't dreamt of her for a while now and if at all possible, I tried not to think about her. It wasn't that I hated her – it was the opposite – I loved her deeply. But to be reminded of her was agony.

The last time I'd seen my mother had been as she'd left the house to go and buy me a birthday cake for my seventeenth birthday party, three years ago. Wearing her favourite summer dress, her black hair swishing about her shoulders, she had waved goodbye to me as she passed through the front garden gate.

"See you later, alligator," she had smiled.

"In a while, crocodile," I smiled back and then added, "I love you!"

Blowing me a kiss, she said, "I love you more." Then she was gone, never to be seen again. By ten o'clock that night, after my father had made several frantic phone calls to friends and family, he called the police. At first they treated her sudden disappearance as a missing person's inquiry, but the longer she stayed away, the more suspicion fell upon my father. She was a cop after all, and they looked after their own. He was taken in for questioning and they kept him there for nearly three days. While he was away, police officers in white suits came to the house and I watched them quietly as they examined every inch of our home. Police officers in black boiler suits turned over the back garden, pulled open the drains, and confiscated our trash. But they found nothing.

My father returned home, looking tired and drawn, white whiskers protruding from his chin. With my arm around him, he sat and sobbed into his hands and I will never forget that. Apart from the disappearance of his wife, he hated being under suspicion of harming her in any way. My father had been devoted to her and as far as I can recall, they had always been close. But more than that, I knew he was hurt by how the police had been so quick to doubt him. For years he had worked alongside them, helping to shed light on the murder victims that so often ended up in his lab.

It was after this that my father was never quite

the same. He was often quiet and he seemed to have lost his appetite and passion for his work. Sure, he still talked about his cases when I asked him, but I could feel his passion for it had gone.

One day as we sat and watched the T.V. together, I looked up at his tired-looking face and said, "You know how you say I can *see* things?"

"Your *gift*," he half-smiled. "What about it?"

"Well it would be a shame if I didn't ever put it to some good use, wouldn't you say?" I asked him.

"It sure would," he said. "What are you planning on doing with it?"

"I'm going to be a cop," I told him, and I'd never been more serious about anything in my life.

"A cop? Just like your mum...*was?*" he said, raising an eyebrow. "She would've been proud of you. Why do you want to be a cop?"

"Because when I do, I'm going to reopen mum's case and I'm gonna find her for you," I told him.

For a moment or two, my father looked as if he didn't know what to say. At first he looked kind of angry and then his face softened and he just looked sad. "That's a wonderful idea, Kiera, but if all those detectives haven't been able to find her after – what's it been now?"

"Eleven months and six days," I said.

"How do you imagine you will be able to find her?" he asked. He wasn't belittling me, he was trying hard not to raise my hopes – and his own, I think.

"Those other detectives might have missed

things," I told him. "They might not have seen all of the clues."

"What clues?" he asked. "There were no clues."

Sitting next to him on the sofa, I said, "There are always clues. You taught me that."

"I know, but this is different -" he started.

Cutting over him, I said, "I know that mum went missing before she even reached the end of our street," I told him.

Pulling away so he could look at me, he said, "Oh come on, Kiera, how could you possibly know that?"

Looking him straight in the eyes, I said, "Mum left the house in her summer dress that day."

"So?"

"Well I remember that day as clearly as if it were yesterday," I told him. "Within a minute or so of her leaving the house, the heavens opened and there was a terrible storm. It lasted a good hour or so. I hadn't seen such heavy rain for a long time. Then there was this really loud thunderclap followed by lightning. It was so loud that I was worried for mum because I knew how scared she got during thunderstorms.

"So knowing that she had only been gone a minute or so and couldn't have even got to the end of the street, I guessed she would've come running back to the house. You know, to either get changed into something waterproof or wait for the storm to pass. But she didn't come back. And taking into account how fussy mum was about keeping her hair nice, the least I would've expected her to do was to come back for a hat. But she didn't. Mum would've never stayed out in that thunderstorm – she would have come back home," I said, looking at him.

Staring back at me, with a sudden look of realisation on his face, he said to me, "My god, Kiera, you're right. So whatever happened to your mum, happened before that storm started?"

"Exactly," I said. "That's how I know she went missing on our very street – just yards from our front door."

"But what could've happened? Where could she have gone in such a short space of time?" he asked.

"That's what I plan to find out," I insisted. "When I become a cop, I'm going to check out her case and read all the statements that were taken from the neighbours in our street. Then when I've read them, I'm going to go visit the neighbours and re-interview them. I know I will *see* something – some small piece of detail – *inconsistencies* – that those other cops didn't *see*. God is in the detail."

"God is in the detail," he repeated, then added, "Did I tell you that?"

"No, mum did," I said and hugged him. "And I promise I will find her for you."

But my father never saw me become a police officer. He died of pancreatic cancer two months before I joined police training school. And that hurt more than everything – it felt as if my heart had been ripped out of my chest. But I intended to keep my promise to him, however long it took me, I would find out what happened to my mother. She was out there somewhere, I knew she was, and my dream only reminded me of that.

Washing away my tears, I left the bathroom. I had to be at the station within two hours. How well Murphy, Potter, and Rom would take my return I didn't know. I would just have to put my trust in Luke.

Remembering that my car still lay in the ditch up on the road, I went to the window to see if the snow had stopped. It had, but it lay in thick drifts along the road and fields that stretched out in front of the Inn. Leaving my police uniform hanging off the back of my chair – not knowing whether to wear it or not after being kicked off the team – I wrapped up warm in a sweatshirt, jeans, and boots. Hitching on my coat, I left my room and immediately noticed the envelope tacked to my door. Taking it down, I opened it and pulled out the folded piece of paper from inside. It was written by the same hand as before. This is what it said:

Luke Bishop is not to be trusted, Kiera.

Folding the note in half, I tucked it into my pocket and headed downstairs.

Chapter Fourteen

I reached the bottom of the stairs, and as I passed the dining area, I heard raised voices coming from the small office behind the bar. Stepping into the shadows by the door, I tried to listen to what was being said. The voices were that of the old woman and her son, Roland, and they were arguing.

"I've had enough, Roland," the old woman croaked. "I can't take it anymore."

"Mother, I've already told you, I can handle it, okay?" Roland snapped.

"We need to leave here," she said, almost seeming to plead with him.

"How many ways have I got to tell you, ma? I've got everything under control!" Roland shouted.

"But what if they come for *us*?" she said, and she sounded frightened. "What if we're next?"

"They won't," he said. "We're safe here."

"There are only so many cloves of garlic I can put up, only so many crucifixes and bottles of holy water I can sell before -" she started.

"Before what, ma?" he cut over her.

"Before there aren't any more people left in this town to protect from -" she hissed.

"I'm done talking about this with you!" he barked. "I know what I'm doing."

Without warning, the office door flew open,

and he stormed from around the bar, heading straight towards me. Slinking back into the shadows, I made myself as small as possible. He passed within a few inches of me. He was so close; I could smell the sweat leaking from his pores.

Once I was certain he'd gone, I crept from my hiding place and headed towards the door. Pulling it open, I heard the old woman's voice behind me. "Don't be forgetting this," she said, tossing me another bottle of holy water.

Snatching it out of the air, and not knowing if she was aware that I'd been eavesdropping, I said, "Thank you."

"You never know when you might need it," she whispered, without smiling.

Turning back towards the door, I heard her say, "If you had half the sense I think you have, you would leave this town and never come back."

Without looking at her, I pushed open the door and sneaked out into the snow with the old woman's warning ringing in my ears. She was right, I should leave, run and keep running and never look back. But I couldn't, and that reason was Luke. Everything he had told me last night had turned my world on its head. Everything that I had learnt – everything I *thought* I knew – was now gone. It was like I was learning from scratch. What I'd seen last night was the stuff of horror movies and fairy tales. But I now knew it was all real. I had been a part of it. I had *become* part of it. Luke was a vampire bat or a *Vampyrus* as he liked to be known. But was there really a difference? There was so much more I needed to find out about him. But wasn't that what had hooked me, the fact that he was a mystery?

When I'd been with Luke the night before, as he had revealed his true self to me, and told me about his world, it was like he had me under a spell, and I kind of just accepted everything he had told me. But now that I was alone and he was away from me, that spell had been broken – a little at least.

Trudging through the snow, hundreds of questions now spiralled through my mind and I didn't have the answers. Was Luke immortal? If not, did he age like a human? Was I safe with him? The note, which had been left for me, came to the forefront of my mind. Could I trust Luke Bishop?

Not knowing the answers to any of these questions, I struggled on towards the town. The pale winter sun was setting, and wanting to be at the police station before nightfall, I quickened my pace. I'd walked a mile or so, when in the distance, I could see something black running towards me in the snow. Stopping, I crouched low, immediately on guard. With my heart racing, I burrowed into a nearby hedgerow. Whatever it was, it was panting as it exhausted and out of breath. With my curiosity getting the better of me, I peeked from my hiding place and almost gasped in relief when I realised what it was coming towards me. Crawling from the snow-laden bush, I stood up and said, "Here boy! Come here!"

Seeing me, the Labrador came bounding

forwards, its huge pink tongue lolling from the corner of its mouth. Recognising it as belonging to the old man I'd spoken with the day before, outside the police station, I took the dog by the collar and patted him. The dog whined and pulled away from me.

"What's up, boy?" I asked it.

Again it whined and pulled in the direction that it had appeared from. Then pulling free of me, it ran back down the road. I chased after it, taking each step as carefully as I could, not wanting to slip and break an arm, or worse, a leg. I didn't fancy lying out in the snow with a broken leg as night started to fall. I thought of those vampires again, and my skin crawled.

Catching up with the dog by a gate in the wall, it stood and barked at me. As I neared it, the dog bounded off again, as if it wanted me to follow. So I did. Making my way across the field, I could see the dog had stopped by something lying in the snow. As I drew near, the Labrador was prodding at it with its snout. He looked back at me and whined.

Approaching the dog, I could see that it was its owner lying face up in the snow. At first, I thought that perhaps the old man had lost his footing while out walking and had collapsed. But as I drew closer, I could see that the snow around him was stained crimson. Following the bloody splash marks, I made my way towards the dead man. I could see tracks around the body, and I was careful not to destroy them. Placing my hands over my mouth, I looked down at the mutilated body. Straight away, I could see that this attack had been far more frenzied than the attack on the Blake boy. That had been bad enough, but this was something else. At least the boy had been left with his face.

The old man lay spread-eagle in the snow. Most of his face and neck had been ripped off. I could see the sinews and muscles that his face had once been attached to. His eye sockets were empty, just two black holes looking back at me. The man's teeth were still intact, but without any lips, he looked as if he were grinning. His jacket and shirt had been slashed in two, revealing his torn-open chest cavity. Several of his ribs had been broken and they stuck out of his chest like white-coloured fingers. His lungs had been half eaten and what was left looked like a pile of pink blancmange. The dog looked at me and whimpered. Reaching out for it, the dog licked what was left of his owner's face, and then ran off into the distance.

Kneeling down, I ran the tips of my fingers over the corpse, my eyes flitting back and forth – unconsciously taking in every minute detail. I dabbed at the blood around the main wound, then the blood further out around the edges, and then the blood that had sprayed over the snow. I got up and paced around the man. Looking left and right, up and down, noting every little thing I could see, almost without knowing that I was doing it. Within seconds, I knew how long ago the killing had taken place, four *people* had taken part, the same three as before, but this time there had been someone new. And the tracks they had left were different – somehow odd. But it wasn't just that. There was something missing. With the light fading fast, I set off back across the field and towards town.

Pushing open the door to the police station, I rushed in. Stamping the snow from my boots, and brushing it from my hair and shoulders, I looked up to see Sergeant Murphy and Constable Potter standing in the office, on the other side of the counter.

"Bishop told us you would come back," Potter said. "He also confessed that you know about…*us*."

"I don't have time for that now…" I started, still out of breath from my hike across the fields to the station.

"He hasn't done you a favour revealing himself to you," Murphy said, coming towards me in that lopsided way of his. "In fact, he's put you in even greater danger."

"I'll worry about that later," I said, trying to catch my breath. "I've found another one."

"Another what?" Potter spat, coming closer.

"Victim," I wheezed. "This one's bad though. It's not like before."

"How?" Murphy asked, his concern undeniable.

"They took his face. I've never seen anything like it. The attack was frenzied – *savage*," I said, and just recalling that mutilated man lying in the snow, made my legs want to buckle beneath me.

Pulling up a chair, Murphy told me to sit down and calm myself. Potter handed me a cup of water and I noted that this was the first kind thing he had done for me since taking up my post in The Ragged Cove.

Once I'd caught my breath, I looked at Murphy and Potter. "There were four of them. They left tracks in the snow. I could have only just missed them."

"By how long?" Potter asked.

"Five minutes," I said, looking at him. Again he rolled his eyes as if dismissing what I'd just said. "Look, blood behaves like many other salty solutions and freezes at between minus two and minus three degrees Celsius," I explained, not wanting to sound as if I were patronising him. "Blood starts to coagulate after less than ten minutes outside of the body, although if you had a shallow pool of blood, it would start to congeal more rapidly around the edges. Temperature also plays a big part. The warmer it is, the slower the coagulation. The colder it is, the faster the coagulation."

Potter and Murphy looked blankly at me.

"It's freezing out there, right?" I said, exasperated. "So if we know that blood clots in less than ten minutes, but more quickly in the cold, the blood on that man was still tacky. My guess is that he couldn't have been murdered more than five minutes before I found his body."

"Where did you learn all this shit?" Potter said.

"It's not shit." I glared at him.

"What else did you *see*?" Murphy asked me, glancing at Potter as if to tell him to be quiet.

"Like I said, they left footprints – four individual sets. But there was something wrong with one of them, I think they had an injury but I can't be sure," I told them.

"Could you see where the tracks led to and from? If we're quick enough, we might be able to track them," Potter said, pulling on his jacket.

"No, it was like before," I said. "There were only tracks around the body – so they must've flown in and out of the crime scene."

"Vampires!" Murphy seethed.

Then looking at the both of them, I said, "Who said anything about vampires?"

"What are you talking about?" Potter said, fixing his utility belt around his waist.

"That man wasn't killed by vampires," I said.

"What then?" Murphy snapped, desperate to find out what I knew.

"Vampyrus," I said. "That man was murdered by *bats*."

"Ridiculous," Potter scoffed. But I noticed the look of concern that flashed between him and his sergeant.

"How can you be certain?" Murphy asked, and I detected a tremor in his voice.

"Like I told you, that man was murdered not long before I discovered him," I started to explain.

"So?" Potter said.

Standing and slapping the palms of my hands against my brow in frustration, I said, "My God, you just don't see it, do you?"

"See what?" Murphy shouted, sounding pissed at me all over again.

"It was still daylight when the killing took

place!" I almost screamed at them. "Vampires can't live in the light, but *Vampyrus* can. But not only that, vampires can't fly!"

"But there was only meant to be the *one*!" Potter said, looking at Murphy. "We were here to track just the one!"

Sergeant Murphy looked at Potter and seemed to be taking in what I'd just said. He was quiet and thoughtful for a moment, and then said, "If the girl is right and we have more than one Vampyrus addicted to the blood of humans, then we've got problems."

"*Problems?*" Potter roared. "If we don't find them – we could have an epidemic!"

"The matter is far worse than I first thought," Murphy said, sucking on the end of his pipe. "Where did you find this body?"

"Do you have a map?" I asked

Without saying anything, Potter pulled one from a desk drawer and spread it out flat.

Looking at the map, I got my bearings, then tracing my finger across it; I stopped at a field about a mile and half from the Crescent Moon Inn. "There," I said. "That's where the body is."

Pulling on his jacket and taking some large flashlights, Murphy and Potter made for the police station door.

"Hang on!" I said to them.

"For what?" Potter asked, looking back at me.

"Where's Luke?"

Glancing at one another, Murphy turned to look

at me and said, "He's gone under."

"Under where?" I asked, my heart beginning to race.

"To the caves," Murphy said, sloping back towards me.

"Home?" I asked, realising that they were talking about The Hollows. "But why?"

"When Rom discovered he had told you everything," Murphy explained, "he sent Luke back below ground."

"But he saved my life," I said.

"He broke the rules," Potter cut in.

"What rules?" I snapped. "That he shouldn't have helped me – *saved* me?"

"He shouldn't have told you about us," Murphy said. "He had no right."

"But he did what he thought was right," I snapped, trying to defend him.

Then, coming towards me, his eyes fixed on mine, and his voice low, Potter said, "Don't be fooled to think that Luke Bishop loves you, Kiera."

"What's that supposed to mean?" I asked staring back; trying not to let the hurt I was feeling show.

"He saved your life to ease his guilty conscience," he said, and half-smiled.

"What's he got to feel guilty about?" I asked, now feeling confused.

Before Potter had a chance to reply, Murphy barked, "Enough Sean! Enough already!"

Slinking away from me as if he'd been bitten, Potter went back to the door where Murphy was waiting for him. "Let's go and sort this mess out," Murphy said.

"What about me?" I asked as they went to leave.

"What about you?" Murphy asked.

"Aren't I coming with you?"

"No," Murphy said. "You'll only slow us down."

"I can lead you straight to the body."

"You don't really think we're going to walk in this weather, do you?" Potter asked, giving me a knowing wink.

God, I hated that guy. "But what am I meant to do here, all on my own?"

"Turn off all the lights and lock all the windows and doors," Murphy said, stepping out into the night. Racing around the counter, I yanked open the door, but the street was deserted, they'd already gone. In the distance, I heard what sounded like two loud thunderclaps.

Chapter Fifteen

Locking the station door behind me, I went back around the front desk to the office. Going to the hatch that led beneath ground, I stood and looked at it. I could see that the hatch had been fastened with a rusty-looking padlock. Was there really another world on the other side of it? A world thousands of years old, where these Vampyrus lived in the utter darkness of caves and caverns?

Stepping away, I saw something glint on the floor just beside the hatch. Bending down, I picked up something small and silver. Half expecting to find another small crucifix, the hairs on the nape of my neck stood on end as I looked at the tiny silver pair of metal wings in my hand. My skin flushed cold as I realised where I'd seen that little parachute regiment tiepin before. It had belonged to the old man I'd met in the street the day before – the old man who now lay dead and mutilated beyond recognition in the field.

But how had it ended up in the police station, just outside the hatch that I had been told led to The Hollows? It was then I realised what had been missing when I'd examined the body – the tiepin. But how then, had it ended up here? Who had brought it to the station and why? Knowing that the four creatures who'd butchered that poor man had all been Vampyrus, my list of suspects wasn't very long.

Then almost stumbling up the corridor, my heart racing in my chest and my stomach clenching, the final missing pictures of that crime scene fitted into place. Not only had the old man's tiepin been missing, so had his walking cane, the one I'd seen him carrying the day before. But why would anyone want to take that? They would've only taken the walking stick if they had needed it to help them...*walk!*

"The footprints! How could you not have seen it, Kiera?" I shouted at myself. That's what was so odd about them. The right footprint of the fourth person present was different because he had been limping!

Hitting me like a flashback, I remembered all of those times I'd seen Sergeant Murphy walking about the office with his right hip sloped down, as if he were limping. Feeling as if I were going to collapse, I gripped the wall. I felt panicked – *scared*. Would Murphy suspect that I knew? And what would he do to me if he did? The same as he'd done to the other cops who had been posted here.

Spinning round as if almost dazed, I knew I had to get as far away as possible from the station – from The Ragged Cove. But how was I to escape and where was I to go? I had no car and the roads were blocked. The phones didn't work, so I couldn't even make contact with the outside world and let them know what was happening. The only place I could go was back to the Inn and lock all the windows and doors – as Potter had said.

But what about him? Had Potter taken part in

the killings? My mind turned to Luke, locked beneath that hatch. Was he like them too – just a killer? My head wasn't sure, but my heart told me no. He had saved me. He'd had plenty of opportunities to kill me if he'd really wanted to, but he hadn't. And I didn't care what Potter had insinuated about him, I knew Luke had feelings for me. Admittedly last night had been weird, but it had been magical, too. I'd never felt those feelings before, like I had with Luke, wrapped inside his wings, my head rested against his chest. The touch of his lips against mine, and the way he had looked into my eyes, as if he were looking into my soul. What were these feelings now burning inside of me? Perhaps if I had ever been in love before, I might have recognised them.

But Luke wasn't going to save me now. I would have to do that myself. Without a way out of The Ragged Cove, I would have to stay and fight. But to do that, I would need as much information as possible about the vampires that had infested the town, and the Vampyrus that worked the vampire shift.

Hurrying around the station, not knowing how long I had before Murphy and Potter returned, I pulled open the desk drawers and filing cabinets. I wasn't sure what I was looking for, but my instincts told me I would know when I found it. I didn't have to wait long; pulling open a set of drawers beneath Sergeant Murphy's desk, I found a bunch of brown cardboard files. Taking them out and placing them on the desk, I thumbed through them. The first had the name 'Police Constable Cooper' typed across the front. Opening it, I found a small picture of a police officer stapled to the paperwork inside. There were some reports and notes written about his service history, but at the back I discovered another sheet of paper that had 'MISSING' stamped across it in blood red letters.

Opening another, I found the same written about an officer named 'Police Constable Munro.' Again, he had been reported missing. Another folder entitled 'Police Constable Ford' contained a picture, and looking at it, I thought I recognised him – but from where? Then, dropping the file as if it had stung me, I realised I had been looking at the human face of the vampire that had attacked me last night, the one in the tattered police uniform.

Gathering the files together, I was just about to put them back where I'd found them, when I saw a folder with 'Police Constable Reeves' written across the front. Picking it up, I opened the folder expecting to find a picture, reports, and service record. But to my surprise, the file was empty. I placed the folders back in Murphy's drawer, exactly as I'd found them.

Turning around, I crossed the office to a set of beat-up looking filing cabinets. Opening them, I found another set of folders, but these were red in colour. Taking out the first, I opened it to find a series of disturbing photos, of a woman whose throat had been shredded. She lay sprawled in a ditch, her hair splayed across her face, eyes open and staring up into the camera lens, as if posing for some grotesque picture. In the file, I found some brief details about her, her name, address, and date of birth. Also recorded was the date and location of her death. The next file contained photos of another murdered victim. This one male, thirty-four years-old. Again I noticed the date and the location of the murder. There were twenty-three files in all, too many for me to read thoroughly. So taking a piece of note paper from a nearby desk, I scribbled down the date of death for each victim, and the location their body had been discovered. Placing the folders back into the filing cabinet, I folded the piece of paper, along with the map, and placed them both into my coat pocket.

Heading back down the corridor, I went to the female locker room. It was more of a cupboard really, as it only had the one locker and the rest of the space was filled with old bikes and other bits of lost property. Reaching into my locker to make sure I'd left nothing behind, as I had no intention of coming back here, I checked each shelf. As I stretched my fingers into the furthest corners, I felt something. Pulling it out, I could see that it was a hairbrush. Knowing it didn't belong to me, I tossed it back onto the shelf, guessing it had been left behind by a previous female officer based at the station.

Turning away, I suddenly stopped. Taking hold of the hairbrush again, I held it up into the light and inspected it. The brush had several blonde hairs snagged around its bristles. Using my fingernails like a set of tweezers, I removed one of the hairs. Looking at it closely, I could see that, just like the hair I'd found in the hand of Henry Blake, this hair had also been dyed peroxide blonde and there was about half an inch of black hair leading from the root.

There was a noise. My heart leapt into my throat and I froze. Fearing that Murphy and Potter had returned, I put the hairbrush back where I'd found it and tiptoed towards the locker room door. Closing it over, leaving just a gap for me to spy through, I looked back down the corridor.

The noise came again, but it wasn't coming from the office – it was closer than that. Pressing my ear to the gap, I listened. The noise sounded like metal clicking, similar to a lock being unpicked. Staring back through the gap again, I could see that it was the padlock on the hatch where the noise was coming from. It jiggled back and forth, making a clunking noise, as if it was being picked open from the other side. With a clink, it fell away from the hatch.

Spying from my hiding place, I watched the hatch swing up and open. There was a sound like a rush of air, as Chief Inspector Rom climbed out and into the corridor. He was naked to the waist, and from his back protruded a set of prehistoric-looking wings. A see-through looking membrane hung from beneath them. His silver hair was swept back from his forehead and he looked up and down the corridor as if checking to see if the coast was clear. Once he was content that he was alone, he looked back into the hole and said, "C'mon, climb up."

Looking in my direction, he held his hand up to whoever was about to appear from the hole, and said, "Wait a minute." Taking several powerful strides, Rom came towards the female locker room. Had he seen me? *Sensed* me? I didn't know, but I had to hide. Glancing around the locker room, I spied the open door of my empty locker and ran towards it. Diving inside, I pulled the door shut as Rom strode into the locker room.

With my heart racing so loud and fast I feared he would hear it, I held my breath. From the other side of the locker door, I could hear the sound of footsteps crossing the room. He stopped, and I didn't know why. Wishing I was someplace else, I closed my eyes and willed him to go away.

Please! I screamed inside my head. *Please don't look inside the locker!*

The sound of his footsteps came closer.

Please no! I begged.

Closer still. My heart was thumping. I held my breath. The door rattled as he took hold of the handle on the other side.

"Rom!" I heard another say, the voice sounding distant. "Rom!"

"I told you to wait," Rom said, his voice sounding angry on the other side of the locker door. I heard the sound of his footsteps heading back across the room.

Covering my mouth with my hands, and closing my eyes, I dropped my head in relief. But I was still in trouble. I had to get out of the police station before Murphy and Potter came back and joined them. Hearing the locker room door close, I waited just to make sure that Rom had gone. When I was certain I couldn't hear him, I eased my way from the locker, being careful not to make any noise.

With my heart pounding in my chest, I crept over to the door. Placing the side of my face against it, I listened. The sound of muffled voices came from the other side. Scraping my long black hair behind my ear, I tried to make out what it was they were saying.

"Bishop has complicated matters," Rom said.

"But he will be dealt with?" the other asked.

With my ear pressed flat against the door, I hoped I might recognise the voice.

"Yes, it is in hand," Rom almost seemed to growl at the other.

There was a pause, then the unknown voice said, "If she were to discover the truth, what then?"

"She already knows about us," Rom said.

"Not that," hissed the other. "I'm talking about if she really knew what happened."

I've already figured it out, wise guy, I thought to myself. *I know it's you who killed the boy and the old man*. But then Rom said something that almost made me drop to the floor in shock.

"This Kiera can't ever find out what happened to her mother," he said.

"Leave that to me," said the other, his voice fading as they walked away down the corridor to the

171

custody block.

Sliding to the floor and pulling my knees up beneath my chin, I sat in numb shock at what I'd just heard. It was as if I'd just woken from a deep sleep – dazed and confused. What did my mother have to do with what was taking place in The Ragged Cove? She had disappeared three years ago on her way to buy me a birthday cake, she had nothing to do with this, I told myself. Perhaps I'd misheard what had been said. But in my heart I knew I hadn't. Why had she come to The Ragged Cove? Who brought her here? But the one thought that ate away at me more than any of the others, was: What had happened to her?

Pulling myself to my feet, I felt sick and frightened. Not for me, but for her. Where was my mother? I felt more determined than ever to uncover what was happening in The Ragged Cove, however dangerous that might be. But I knew I had little time left before the Vampyrus, the vampires, or both came for me.

Listening against the door to make sure Rom and his companion were not on the other side, I slowly turned the handle. Opening it just a fraction, I put my eye to the crack and peered out. The corridor was empty and the hatch was closed, fastened again with the rusty padlock. In the distance, I could hear the sound of voices. Opening the door another inch, I listened. It was the sound of them talking. Their voices hollow and coming from the custody block.

Sneaking from behind the door, I stepped into

the corridor. With their voices fading behind me, I glanced down again at the hatch. Through its metal grating, I could see only darkness as it spiralled away into hell. Reaching the main office, I crept around the front counter, unlocked the door, and left the police station.

It had started to snow again, and with no other option but to return to the Crescent Moon Inn, I set off towards it. I just prayed I could reach it before either the vampires or Vampyrus took me.

Chapter Sixteen

With the Crescent Moon Inn within sight, I ran as fast as I could towards it. It had taken me over an hour to walk from the police station and every minute had seemed like an eternity. It hadn't just been the freezing snow that had made my journey so miserable; it had been the constant fear that at any moment, I would be rushed at by screaming vampires or snatched into the air by flying Vampyrus. With Luke banished to The Hollows, I felt exposed and unprotected. I wondered now if he could be trusted, and although I'd refused to dwell earlier on Potter's comments about Luke's guilt, I now feared what he might have to feel guilty about.

Ever since overhearing Rom mention my mother, I knew that whatever had happened to her, the Vampyrus had been involved and I feared Luke had played a part in that.

Reaching the Inn, I pushed open the door and stepped inside. The bar area had the usual number of locals clustered around the tables, warming themselves by the fire, cradling a neat whiskey in their hands. Again, they all looked up at me and the room fell into a hushed silence. I felt like screaming at them, *WHAT ARE YOU ALL LOOKING AT?* But I didn't. I skulked across the bar with my head down, just wanting to get tonight over with. As I reached the foot of the staircase leading up to the bedrooms, Roland appeared in the doorway of the small back office. I jumped, his sudden presence making me gasp. He looked at me, his jowls glowing red, as he wiped his meaty hands against his stained apron.

"I'm sorry, I didn't mean to alarm you," he blushed.

"It's okay," I said, forcing a smile.

"Well if you are sure…"

"I'm sure," I told him, just wanting to get to my room.

"It's just that you look washed-out – *ill*," he said.

"It's been one of those days." I knew he was only trying to be nice, but I wasn't in the mood for him.

"Perhaps, I could fix you up with something to eat?" he smiled. "A sandwich, perhaps?"

"I thought your mother was strict about eating times?" I said, unzipping my coat. It had been freezing outside, but with the heat from the roaring fire coming from the bar, the Inn felt hot and oppressive.

"Don't take any notice of mother," he smiled. And then leaning in towards me, he whispered, "She has her odd little ways."

I hadn't been so close to Roland before, and as he stepped forward, I could see beads of sweat lining his brow and glistening on his upper lip. His eyes looked puffy and his lips tinged blue. Seeing that his circulation was obviously bad, I guessed that he would be dead of a heart attack by the time he was fifty. It was hard to tell how old he was as his plumpness consumed any wrinkles or lines his face might have. His dark, wavy hair was messy and dirty, combed back, and greasy-looking. His chubby hands were flecked with blood from where he had been preparing raw meat in the kitchen. His breath smelt bad and the thought of him preparing any food for me was repulsive.

Inching my way up the stairs, I looked back at him and said, "It's really sweet of you to offer, Roland, but I just want to get some sleep."

"If you're sure, young lady," he called after me. "I really don't mind."

"Thank you," I called back over my shoulder, "but I'm sure. Goodnight, Roland."

Closing my bedroom door behind me, I threw off my coat, and taking the map and the list of the dates and locations of the murders, I sat on the floor. Spreading the map before me, I took a pen and made a mark on the map, highlighting where the murders furthest apart had taken place. I'd often heard my father talk about studies he had read of murders committed by serial killers. There were several theories stating that most serial killers committed their murders close to their home address. It often took less effort on the part of the killer if they committed their crimes close to home, and they liked to be a minimum distance away from their home so they could return there quickly once the crime had been committed. I heard dad say once that if you took the two furthest locations of the killers crimes, marked them on a map and drew a circle around them, somewhere in that ring you would have your killer.

So with my pen, I drew a large circle on the map. But I knew that I wasn't dealing with just one killer, I was dealing with several – possibly more. But I had a theory of my own. Luke had told me that when the *hunger* was upon them, it was like a burning sensation in their very souls, which couldn't be satisfied unless they gave into it or returned back to The Hollows and waited for it to subside. They were like drug addicts or those who were starving. And in either case, would an addict walk miles for a fix if they knew they could get one close by? Would someone who was starving walk past several restaurants, or go and eat at the first one they came across? The same rules applied to the Vampyrus and the vampires. When they woke and their craving was at its height, they would kill and eat from the first available source of food they came across.

So taking my list, I marked on the map every location and the date that a victim had been found. Once I'd finished, I sat back and looked at the map. In the centre, there was a cluster of tiny crosses. These marked the killings furthest back in time. Then as I reached the most recent murders, the crosses spread further out over the map until they touched the edge of the circle that I'd made.

But why would the killings be taking place further and further away from the centre of the ring, I wondered. Then thinking of the little old woman downstairs and her bottles of holy water, crucifixes, and decorations made of garlic, I realised why the murders had been taking place further out of town. As the news of the body count had grown, and with it the rumours of vampires, the residents of The Ragged Cove had taken precautions by stocking up on holy water, crucifixes, and decorating their homes with cloves of garlic. So as more and more of the terrified villagers had done this, the further away the Vampyrus and vampires had to go to find victims and sedate their hunger. Thinking of how I'd been attacked on the town's border, it suggested to me that my hypothesis was right. How many homes would those vampires had to have passed, all of them filled with humans and their delicious blood, before they came across me? There would have been hundreds, but each night they had been pushed further and further afield in search of food. But as they did, they were spreading their net beyond the reaches of The Ragged Cove, and with every killing, another vampire was born.

Realising that time was running out if I were to…to do what exactly? I didn't know. But to know the location of their lair would be a start. So looking back at the map, I stuck the tip of my pen in the centre of the group of concentrated crosses. Pulling it away again, I looked at the mark it had made on the top of St. Mary's Church. Reeling in shock and disbelief, I slumped backwards onto my butt and stared down at the map. Before I'd had time to fully comprehend what I'd discovered, I noticed a shadow beneath my bedroom door as if someone were standing outside it. Believing

Roland had ignored my refusals to take up his offer of something to eat; I got up and went to the door.

Yanking it open, I said, "Look, Roland, it really is very sweet of you but -" Before I'd had a chance to finish, I realised that it wasn't the Innkeeper standing outside my room, but the hooded man who had been leaving me the envelopes and crucifixes.

We both gasped at the same time, me in shock and him as if he really didn't want to get caught. Sensing this, I grabbed for him, desperate to know who had been following me since my arrival at The Ragged Cove. He jumped back away from me, but he wasn't quick enough and I had hold of his hoodie. He pushed me in the chest, and I fell backwards into my room, crashing to the floor and taking him with me. Rolling onto my back, I watched him get up and bolt for the door. Reaching out with both arms, I wrapped them around his legs. Toppling over like a stack of children's bricks, he slammed into the floor again. Kneeling on his chest, pinning him down, I pulled back the hood. Recognising the face that stared back at me, I jumped back and gasped, "What are you doing here?"

Chapter Seventeen

"Covering your back," Sergeant Phillips groaned, looking up at me from beneath the hood.

"Why?" I asked, still shocked at discovering the hooded man was my sergeant from training school.

"Why do you think?" he said, getting up off the floor. "You might have noticed that this town ain't exactly normal."

"Then why send me here?" I asked, sitting on the edge of my bed.

"No one sent you," Phillips said. "You volunteered, remember?"

"With plenty of persuasion from you," I reminded him as he sat down at the desk.

"Okay, okay," he said, "However it happened, you're here now and in incredible danger."

"I've worked that out for myself," I told him.

"You only know the half of it," he said, his voice lowered.

"What do you mean, Sarge?" I said, fearing what he had to tell me.

"For starters, stop calling me Sarge," he half-smiled. "We're not at training school now."

"Sorry, Craig," I said, feeling odd calling him by his first name. He was kind of handsome, in his mid-thirties, but had gone prematurely grey – white - if I were to be honest. But it kind of suited his rugged looks and gave him a look of authority, almost imposing. I hadn't exactly had a *thing* for him as a recruit, but I had made a complete fool of myself on graduation day. I'd been upset and hurt that my father had died just a few months before my joining the police force. At the evening function, the women dressed in their gowns and the men in their tuxedoes, I'd consumed one too many glasses of wine and my grief had overtaken me.

Wanting to be held and comforted, I'd smooched up to Sergeant Phillips and draped my arm around him. The rest is kind of a blur, but I did have vague memories of trying to entice him onto the dance floor. When he'd refused, I told him how hot he looked in his tuxedo and asked if he had a wife. The next thing I remember was waking the next morning in my small room, lying on top of my bed, still wearing my ball gown and cradling a picture of my father to my chest.

Embarrassed, I'd asked my colleagues what had happened and they told me that I'd collapsed in the middle of the dance floor, where I'd sat and cried for my father. Swooping me up into his arms, they told me how Sergeant Phillips had carried me back to my room and put me to bed. For the next few days, it was hard looking him in the eyes, but he had been decent about it and hadn't mentioned it since.

"How much do you know?" he asked, yanking me from my memories of him.

"I know that this town isn't *normal*," I told him.

"What do you mean?" he asked, leaning forward in his seat.

"The cops in this town – how can I put this?" I said, knowing what I had to say would seem unbelievable. "Well they're not like regular cops. They're not like you and me."

"Of course they are," he said. "I've known Sergeant Murphy, Potter, and Bishop for years."

"You don't know them as well as I do then," I assured him. "And besides, if you know and trust them all so well, why did you leave me a note telling me that I shouldn't trust Luke?" I asked him, needing to know what it was that Luke had to feel guilty about. But more than that, I needed to know if my trust in him had been misplaced, and if his feelings for me had been real.

Shifting in his seat, Craig leant into me, as if what he had to tell me was such a grave secret he couldn't afford to let anyone else overhear it.

"It has to do with your mother," he said, just above a whisper.

Believing I'd misheard him, I said, "Sorry, what did you say?"

"It is believed that Luke Bishop played some part in your mother's disappearance," he said, searching my eyes to gauge my reaction.

"But how?" I mumbled, desperate to make sense of what he was telling me. Knowing that Luke was a Vampyrus, I said to Craig,
"Did he murder her?"

"Not exactly," he said.

"What's that supposed to mean?" I snapped, jumping up from the edge of my bed. "What was my mother doing in this town anyhow?"

Sensing I was getting stressed, Craig looked at me, and in a calm and almost soothing voice, he said, "Please, Kiera, sit down and I'll tell you everything I know."

Sitting again, Craig said, "There have been killings taking place in this town for a few years now. At first they were sporadic and believed to have been committed by wild animals, the wounds inflicted on the victims all suggested that. Then the grave desecrations started occurring and people started to go missing. The stories started to get a lot of media attention and the whole thing turned into some kind of circus for a while. Rumours started to spread that the town was infested with vampires, but of course this theory was never taken seriously.

"Murphy and his small team were posted here. It became obvious they weren't making much progress. So it was decided that some of our most brightest and resourceful officers should be posted here to help investigate the crimes. But one by one, they went missing, seeming to disappear off the face of the Earth. Headquarters was at its wits end. Your mother had gained herself a reputation as being a maverick who had the uncanny intuition to solve crimes that had left other officers – often more experienced and senior in rank – baffled and confused.

"Many times your mother had been approached to join the National Crime Squad, but each time she had declined, saying that although she loved her job, her main love was for you and your father and she didn't want to do anything that might cause her to spend too much time away from you both.

"But with pressure on us to solve the murders in The Ragged Cove, a certain amount of pressure was put on her to change her mind," he said.

"What sort of pressure?" I asked him.

Looking down at his feet as if he were ashamed of what he had to tell me, he said, "Some drugs that had been recovered from a raid a few weeks before were found in her locker."

"But my mother wouldn't have ever taken drugs -" I shouted in her defence.

Before I'd the chance to finish, Craig said, "You don't have to try and convince me. Your mother was set up – blackmailed into coming down here. It was explained to her that if she came to The Ragged Cove, then the drugs found in her locker would magically disappear and nothing more would ever be said about them. But if she refused, then she would be arrested and charged, leaving her career in ruins. Your mother was switched on enough to know that if she were imprisoned for drug possession, not only would it have had a damaging effect on your father's reputation, but it would have also destroyed you."

"So having no real choice, she agreed to go to The Ragged Cove, but on the condition that it would be for two weeks only. It was agreed, and knowing your mother's ability to solve the most complex of crimes, two weeks was considered to be long enough. But she was sworn to secrecy. Your mother was to tell no one where she was going or what she was doing," Craig explained.

"Why not?" I asked.

"Each of the other officers sent here had gone missing as you know," he said, "so we wondered if there was some link between force headquarters and whoever was committing the murders in the town. We needed it to look like she had just been sent as part of a routine attachment. We changed her name and collar number, and she even changed her appearance. No one was to know that she'd been sent as part of the investigation team. That's why your mother had to vanish that day three years ago," he explained.

"So if you knew my mother had gone on some undercover assignment here, why was my father arrested, our home and garden searched?" I asked, growing evermore angry in the knowledge that we had been lied to for all these years.

"Only a few people knew at headquarters," he said, "so your mother's disappearance was treated just like any other."

"But they *arrested* my father!" I almost screamed at him. "He was never the same man after that. My father had been a proud man, but after the finger-pointing and accusations, he changed. And I think it was that stress and not knowing what had happened to my mother – *his wife* – that led to him dying so young."

"You've got to understand, Kiera, it wasn't my

decision," Craig said, and he didn't look me in the eyes.

"No, but you knew about it!" I hissed at him, any respect that I'd previously had for him, fast disappearing. "You went along with it!"

"No one could've known what would've happened to your mother," he said.

"Oh, come on!" I snapped. "You must have had a pretty good idea! After all, every other cop you sent to this godforsaken place had gone missing."

"But we believed it would be different this time around – your mother was *different*," he insisted, looking up at me.

"So what did happen to her?" I asked.

"We're not exactly sure'" he confessed.

"Not exactly sure?" I roared. "This just keeps getting better and better!"

"We suspect Luke Bishop was involved," he said.

'How?' I snapped, part of me not wanting to hear that Luke could have somehow been involved in my mother's disappearance.

"He was crewed up with her the night she vanished," Craig said. "He was interviewed but could give no explanation as to what had happened to her. He said they attended the scene of one of those murder victims. Apparently, he had gone off into the woods on his own to investigate some noises he'd heard, leaving your mother at the scene. He said he returned a short time later, only to find that she had gone," Craig said.

Remembering how Luke had suddenly

disappeared on the night we'd been at the graveyard, my heart sank. "He did the same to me," I told Craig. "We went up to St. Mary's Church to investigate a grave that had been desecrated. I climbed down into the hole to take a better look, but when I came up he'd gone. In his place was a young girl. I called over the radio for him, but he never answered. Time and time again, I called for him to back me up, but he was nowhere to be found. Not until it was all over did he reappear."

"Why were you calling for backup?" Craig asked.

"The girl was a vampire," I told him, not caring if he believed me or not.

"Did I hear you right?" he said. "Did you just say *vampire*?"

"You heard right the first time," I replied. "Believe it or not, Craig, this town is teaming with them."

"Half of me had begun to suspect the rumours were true. That's why I left you the crucifixes, but..." he started, and then trailed off as if lost for words.

"I know, it's the stuff of horror movies and nightmares. I didn't believe it myself at first, but when you have one climbing all over your police car trying to rip your face off, it gives you a different perspective on things," I said.

Craig must have seen the haunted look in my eyes as I recalled what happened at the graveyard, because he looked at me and said, "You're not kidding, are you?"

"Why would I want to lie about something like that?" I asked. "I risk my whole career just by telling you."

Craig slumped forward on the chair and studied my face. The silence seemed to stretch out forever. When I thought he was just about to get up and leave, he said, "Kiera, if anybody else had told me such a thing, I'd be taking their badge and telling them to get themselves some therapy. But I know you, I know how methodical your mind works and how you are only ever interested in the facts, in what you can *see* and touch."

"I've seen and touched things that I would never have believed possible," I told him. "But it's not only that; I have some feelings for Luke."

Craig didn't say anything. He just sat and stared, leaving me to come to my own conclusions. "If you don't trust him," I said, "If you think that in some way he is involved in the killings, why is he still a cop?"

"We have no proof," Craig said. Then staring me straight in the face, he added, "That's where you come in."

"How?"

"You weren't just chosen to come to The Ragged Cove because of the abilities you share with your mother," he said.

"Why else then?" I asked him.

"Kiera, you're a beautiful woman. Most men would give up their souls to be with you," he said. "Take a look at yourself. You've long, jet-black hair, eyes the colour of honey, and a mouth that most men would happily die trying to kiss."

His compliments didn't embarrass me or make me blush, they made me angry. "So what you're saying is – I was nothing more than bait!" I said, through clenched teeth. "You got me down here to flush him out. You hoped we would fall for each other and he would open up to me?"

"And has he?" Craig asked. "Is he the link between the disappearing officers and these *vampires*?"

Looking at Craig with a wistful smile on my lips, I said, "Oh yeah, he opened up alright but not in the way you think."

"What do you mean?" Craig asked, looking confused.

"Luke Bishop isn't human!" I shouted at him. "He's a Vampyrus!"

"What's that?" Craig asked. "Some kind of vampire?"

"No, he's not a vampire. He did tell me the proper name, desmondus something-or-another – I can't remember now," I said. "But anyway, translated it means the Vampyrus are a breed of vampire bat!"

Standing, Craig laughed, "You're joking, right? I mean, you're making this up?"

"Look, I don't have time to stand here making up fairy tales," I snapped. "He showed me his wings -"

"*Wings?*" Craig cut in.

"*Listen to me!*" I yelled at him. "He can fly at incredible speeds, he's strong – I mean I saw him tear vampires in half like they were scraps of paper!"

"Look, I'm getting lost here," Craig said. "So what's the difference between a vampire and whatever you say Bishop is?'

"The Vampyrus have always been here," I tried to explain. "What I mean is, they were here before us humans. They live beneath us in caves and caverns. But during the course of human history, some have come above ground and have decided to live among us. Like vampires, they do crave human blood, but usually they go back beneath ground whenever the hunger is on them and sweat it out."

"Like a drug addict going cold turkey?" Craig asked.

"I guess," I said. "Anyway, some of them have given into those cravings and have started to kill and feed off humans. But the humans they kill don't really die; they come back as vampires – like a mutant form of the Vampyrus. They don't have wings like Luke…"

"Kiera, how can I put this," he said, "I've never seen Luke Bishop with wings. I'm sure I would've noticed –"

"You're not listening to me!" I yelled, slamming my fists against my thighs with frustration. "They change! You can't always see their wings. Most of the time they look just like us."

"*Their* wings?" Craig said.

"Luke's not the only one."

"There are others?" Craig asked, as if he were trying to catch up with what I was telling him.

"Murphy, Potter, and Rom, they're all vampire bats."

"Rom?" Craig gasped. "You must be mistaken."

"I'm not," I insisted. "I saw him only a couple of hours ago and he looked like he had wings to me."

"But Rom is the one who sent your mother here," he told me, his eyes growing wide. "He was the one who blackmailed her…"

"Believe me now?" I asked, as everything seemed to fall into place for him.

"I don't want to," he whispered. "It's just that…"

"What?"

"This is a lot worse than I could've ever imagined," he said and looked at me.

"It gets a lot worse," I told him.

"How?"

"I think I've worked out where the vampires' lair is," I replied. "It's at -"

But before I could finish, Craig cut in and said, "The church?"

"How did you know that?" I asked.

"I'm one step ahead of you, Kiera," he half-smiled. "You saw me up at the graveyard the other day, right?"

"Right."

"Well, while I've been down here keeping an eye out for you, I've been doing some investigating myself," he told me. "After I learnt about the girl's grave being desecrated, I decided to stake it out, just in case there was any truth in these vampire rumours. The priest, Father Taylor, caught me in the graveyard and asked what I was doing. I told him I had an interest in church architecture. I asked him if I could have a look around, but he said it was inconvenient as he was about to attend mass. Anyway, he agreed to show me around today, but never showed up. I waited for an hour or more. His rapidly depleting parishioners showed up for afternoon mass, but he didn't. I'm beginning to fear that he has become another victim or one of these vampires."

"Or Vampyrus," I added.

"Fancy checking it out?" he asked, his eyes wide.

"One step ahead of you, Sarge," I said, pulling on my coat. "I'd already decided to go up there just before you showed up."

Chapter Eighteen

Entering the bar area of the Inn, I could see that most of those who had stared at me earlier had now drifted back out into the cold to make their way home. There were just a couple of barflies sitting by the fire.

"You know, I don't have any of my equipment on me," Craig said. "If things start to turn ugly up at the church, we should have our -"

Cutting over him, I said, "Forget it. CS spray and Tasers aren't going to be any good against vampires."

"What then?" he asked. "We can't go unprotected."

Then, turning towards the little table that housed all the old woman's bottles of holy water and crucifixes, I scooped some up and handed them to Craig. "Fill your pockets with these," I told him. "Believe it or not, the crucifix you left for me worked."

"You're kidding me," he said.

"Do I look like I'm joking?" I said, holding out my hands that were visibly shaking at the thought of what had happened that night with Kristy Hall.

"I guess not," he replied, and began to stuff his pockets with the religious items.

Taking all of the old woman's supplies, I filled all of my coat pockets and headed towards the door. The cold outside hit me like a slap in the face. Burying my head low and thrusting my hands into my jeans pockets,

I looked at Craig and said, "Ready?"

"Ready," he answered, pulling his hood over his head as we set off in the direction of the church.

Snow came down so hard and fast, it was like we were walking in a blizzard, and I couldn't help but think back to the night I'd become disorientated in the fields and been attacked by the vampires. I thought of Luke again and my heart ached. Despite what Craig had told me about him, a tiny part of me didn't want to give up on him. All I could think about was how he had rescued me that night. I could feel that warm sensation pass over me again, as I remembered his touch, his kisses, and how he had held me so close to him. Reminding myself of all of that, I couldn't – *or didn't* - want to believe he had played any part in my mother's disappearance. If he had, then he had cheated me – used me – cast me under some kind of spell so that I hadn't been able to *see* his treachery.

"What are you thinking about?" Craig asked over the howl of the bitter wind.

Not wanting to tell him about the confusing feelings and misgivings I had about Luke, I lied. "I was wondering what you were doing outside my room tonight."

"Just checking up on you," he said, waving snow away from in front of his eyes. "I take a drink some nights in the bar, then pretending I need to use the bathroom, I sneak upstairs and just listen, you know, to make sure you're alright."

"So why the disguise?" I asked him.

"I didn't agree with Rom's decision to send you here," he said. "I asked him if I could come with you, you know, just to keep an eye on things, especially after what had happened to your mother. He refused, so I took a few weeks annual leave that were due to me. I couldn't risk being discovered by anyone, because if it had gotten back to Rom that I'd disobeyed his orders, I would've been in all kinds of crap."

Discovering Craig had put so much at risk for me, I gently squeezed his arm and thanked him.

"No problem," he smiled, as the snow swirled all around us.

We walked in silence for a time; the only sound was the wind screaming in off the fields. I would be lying if I said I wasn't scared of what might lay ahead for us, but I knew that whatever danger faced me, I would have to confront it. I'd made a promise to my father and I intended on keeping it. Thinking of my mother again, I said, "So what was my mother's secret name?"

With his head turned against the falling snow, Craig glanced sideways at me and said, "Police Constable Jessica Reeves."

Hearing him say the name 'Reeves', I thought of the empty file I'd discovered back at the police station, along with all the other records kept about the missing police officers. But all of the others had reports and a photograph inside. Why had my mother's file been empty? Perhaps it was because there were no reports to send. After all, *Police Constable Jessica Reeves*, didn't really exist. But wouldn't the whole scenario have been more believable if they had created some fictitious records for her? If Rom had gone to the trouble of planting drugs in her locker, then surely he could've taken the time to write up a few fake reports?

Looking sideways at Craig, I said, "You told me my mother had to change her appearance."

"That's right," he nodded.

"She dyed her black hair blonde, didn't she," I said.

Glancing at me through the falling snow, he asked, "How did you know?"

Thinking of the hairbrush I'd found in my locker with the dyed blonde hairs and black roots, I said, "It doesn't matter." But the hairbrush hadn't been the only place I'd found those hairs. I'd found them in Henry Blake's tiny, dead hand. That was only two days ago, which meant my mother was still alive and somewhere in The Ragged Cove. Realising this, I wanted to scream, dance, and punch the air with joy. But then another thought came to me, and my heart felt as if it were being crushed within my chest. What were strands of my mother's hair doing in the hand of that dead boy? Before I'd had the chance to consider how the hair had got there, Craig, was tugging on my sleeve and pointing into the distance.

"See the church?" he asked.

I looked ahead, and through the blizzard, I could see the steeple of the church spiralling upwards like a black scratch on the overcast sky.

"Do you think this stuff will work?" Craig asked,

patting his pocket containing the holy water and crucifixes.

"It did last time," I mumbled, my teeth now chattering with the cold.

"Ok then," he said, setting off towards the church. I followed him through the gate and up the gravel path. Reaching the doors at the front of the church, Craig pulled down on the handle and pushed. With a wailing sound, the door creaked open and we stepped inside.

Chapter Nineteen

The draft from the open doorway caused the candlelight to flicker, sending long, dark shadows up the inside of the church. The church was silent, and its thick stone walls muffled the sound of the howling wind outside. From inside, the wind sounded like children weeping.

The smell of wax was sweet and seemed almost intoxicating. Taking my hands from my pockets, I blew warm breath over them. Wiggling my fingers, I tried to get some feeling back. My nose and ears felt numb as well, and my hair was wet with melting snow. Walking between the rows of pews, my boots made a whispering sound against the hard stone floor. I looked over my shoulder to see where Craig was. He was taking two candles from beneath a statue of the Virgin Mary.

"Take one of these," he said, holding out the candle towards me, and even though he had whispered, his voice echoed around the church.

Weaving between the pews, I made my way towards him. Taking one of the candles, I said, "You can take your hood off now."

"You must be joking," he said. "It's freezing in here." Then holding a candle out before him, he said, "Let's see what's down here."

I followed Craig to a set of grey stone steps that spiralled downwards into the darkness beneath the church. "What do you reckon?" he said, looking back at me over his shoulder.

"About what?" I asked him.

"Does this seem the sorta place that vampires would hang out?" he said from beneath his hood.

"How should I know?"

"I thought you were the expert," he whispered.

"If what you're trying to tell me is that you're scared, sergeant, then I'll go first," I said, brushing past him and making my way down the spiral staircase.

"That's not what I was saying at all," his voice echoed, followed by the sound of his footsteps as he rushed after me.

Taking one step at a time, I made my way down into the darkness. Even though I held the candle with both hands, it still shook from side to side as I trembled in fear at what might be hiding below. The stairs seemed never-ending, spiralling around and around like a corkscrew, burying itself into the earth. Craig was right behind me and he took short, shallow breaths. I guessed we were nearing the bottom of the stairwell, as not only had the air grown colder, it was damper, too. In the candlelight, I could see mould growing down the walls and the *plink-plink-plink* sound of water dripping in the distance.

Looking down, I could see the last couple of steps levelling out into a narrow tunnel. Like everything else around me, the tunnel had been chiselled out of the rock and earth below ground. Without enough room in the tunnel to walk side by side, we had to walk single-file, with me leading. We hadn't been going long when the light from my candle seemed to fade. It hadn't gone out – it had dimmed. It took me a few seconds to realise that we had stepped from the tunnel into a huge, open chamber. It was so vast and black that the darkness surrounding us seemed to be sucking up the light from our candles.

Craig came and stood next to me, and even with the light from both of our candles, it did nothing to penetrate the black wall of darkness in front of us. The blackness almost seemed to reach out and touch me. It was like it wanted to smother me, suffocate me. The silence was deafening and the only noise I could hear was the frantic beating of my own heart.

"Craig," I whispered.

"Yes?"

"Where are we?"

"In my lair," said a voice, but it wasn't Craig's. The voice came from in front of me, only a few feet away. It was so sudden and unexpected I flinched and screamed all at the same time.

"Craig, are you there?" I called and reached out into the darkness.

"I'm here," he said, sounding only inches away and taking my hand.

"Did you hear that?" I whispered, my voice broken with fear.

"Of course he heard it, my child," the voice came again, and it sounded soft and soothing – the sort of voice you would like to read you a bedtime story as a child.

"Who's there?" I asked, my voice wavering.

Almost as if in reply to my question, there was a scratching sound, as a match was scratched into life. It flared for a moment, its sudden brightness blinding me in the dark. The light winked back and forth as a candle was lit. The flame steadied and in its orange glow, I could see a face staring back at me out of the darkness. It was the eyes that I recognised first, the fierce sparkle of blue in them.

"Welcome, Kiera Hudson," said Father Taylor. "You are very welcome in my church."

"What are you doing down here?" I asked, some of my fear ebbing away on realising that it was just the old priest I'd met on my visit to the graveyard with Luke.

Ignoring my question, he said, "I'm sorry it's so dark down here. Let's see if I can remedy that."

I watched his flame flicker to and fro as he lit several other candles. As light seeped into the crypt, I could see that there were candles on tall, silver stands all around him. Father Taylor was seated in a high-backed cushioned chair. Although he had lit several of the candles, it wasn't bright enough to penetrate the darkness that surrounded him.

"That's better," he smiled, settling back into his chair.

"What are you doing down here?" I asked again.

"Waiting," he smiled, his drawn cheeks looking

even more hollowed than I remembered them to be.

"Waiting for what?" I asked, glancing at Craig in the hope he might know what the priest was talking about.

"Why for you, of course," Father Taylor smiled again.

Sensing there was something terribly wrong about all of this, I let go of Craig's hand and started to edge backwards towards the tunnel.

"You don't have to be afraid," the priest smiled again, holding out his hand for me to take. "You're in a church. Where could you be safer?"

"Craig, something's wrong here," I whispered into the dark.

"I think he's okay," he whispered back. "He's just an old guy."

"Tsk, tsk, Sergeant Phillips," the priest grinned. "You haven't explained to her yet why she is really here?"

"Craig?" I said my heart beginning to race all over again. "What's he talking about? What haven't you explained to me?"

"I'm sorry, Kiera," Craig said, turning towards me.

"For what?" I asked, now utterly confused.

"He's not really sorry," Father Taylor answered for him.

Looking back at the priest, I watched as he got up from his seat. He wobbled just slightly as if trying to catch his balance. It was then I remembered him limping away from Craig the day I spied on them both from behind the gravestone. Then, taking a walking cane he had rested against his chair, he shuffled towards me. My heart skipped a beat and my stomach tightened, for even in the darkness, I knew the cane belonged to the old man I'd discovered mutilated beyond recognition in the field. Its silver ornate top twinkled in the candlelight.

"It wasn't Murphy," I whispered to myself.

"What did you say, my dear?" he smiled, edging his way closer towards me.

"It was you all along," I gasped, realising the mistake I'd made.

"Get away from me," I hissed, stumbling backwards.

"Wait, Kiera," Craig said, turning towards me.

"For what?" I said, backing into the tunnel.

"To see what you could become," he half-smiled at me.

"To see *what*?" I asked.

Then something strange happened. Behind Father Taylor I could see shapes. How was that possible? There was only blackness behind him, solid blackness. But somehow I could *see* into it – *through it*. It was like I was *seeing* for the very first time.

You have a gift, I remembered my father telling me. *You can see things others can't.*

Looking into the darkness behind the priest, I could see shapes coming closer. They were people. I blinked and when I looked again it was like flashbulbs popping on and off in the darkness. I was seeing quick, blinding glimpses of those who were hiding in the blackness all around me. And in each of those snapshots, I saw their white, misshapen faces, their dead eyes, and drooling fangs. I was surrounded by vampires.

As quickly as they had come, those snapshots were gone and it was like I couldn't *see* anymore. Dazed and confused by what had just happened, I steadied myself against the mouth of the tunnel. Father Taylor and Craig were coming towards me, the candles they were holding lighting up their faces like Halloween pumpkins.

Looking at Craig, I said, "I trusted you! I thought you were my friend! You didn't leave those crucifixes because you cared – you just didn't want the vampires to get me before you did!"

Turning, I raced into the tunnel. Within seconds my candle had snuffed out and I ran blindly into the darkness. Behind me, I could hear the sound of running feet and screeching. Snatching a quick look back over my shoulder, there was only blackness again. Facing front, I raced on, my hands stretched out before me as I felt my way out. The sound of racing footsteps and screaming got closer and I pushed on. My lungs felt as if they were ablaze inside of me, and my heart pounded against my chest.

Faster! I screamed inside my head. *Faster!*

Adrenaline surged through my whole body as the sound of those chasing me grew ever nearer. But it wasn't just the sound of feet and shrieking I could hear echoing through the tunnel behind me. There was a scratching, scuttling noise too, as if some of those racing after me were crawling along the walls and the ceiling of the tunnel.

Something struck my foot and I fell forward onto the ground. Blindly reaching out with my hands, I felt the first step of the spiral staircase. Realising it was that which had tripped me, I scrambled up them. Trailing my fingers along the wall to keep my bearings in the complete darkness, I headed upwards. The sound of feet on the stairs coming after me grew ever closer. My calf muscles throbbed as I tried to leap two steps at a time. But I was slowing, and those behind me sensed it and sped up.

Fingers curled around my ankle and yanked me backwards. Spilling forward, I slammed into the stone steps, squeezing the air from my lungs.

"Kiera," I heard Craig whisper from out of the darkness.

Kicking out frantically with my legs, I screamed, but my lungs were still empty and the noise I made sounded as if I was being strangled. My foot connected with something in the darkness and I heard Craig shriek out in pain and anger. His fingers loosened around my ankle, and seizing my chance, I pulled away and started back up the stairs on my hands and knees.

Feeling my way around the curved wall of the stairwell, my heart raced at the glimmer of light coming from above me. Knowing it was the church, I made one last desperate surge upwards. As I got nearer to the light, the darkness around me began to fade, and illuminated the true horror of what was behind me.

Looking back over my shoulder, I could see Craig charging up the stairwell, followed by a hoard of frenzied-looking vampires. Some of them ran, but others scurried up the walls like freaky-looking spiders, their jaws snapping open and closed, spraying the walls with spit and froth which hung from their razor-sharp teeth. Their hair was matted with blood and grime and they looked crazed. With eyes seething red in their hideous faces they lunged for me, claws just inches from my exposed flesh. I launched myself up the last few steps and bounded into the church. Racing towards the door, I heard the sound of the creatures pouring out of the stairwell behind me. Pews were pushed out of the way and reduced to splinters, the sounds of their screams deafening.

Reaching the church door, I fumbled for the handle. Yanking on it with all my remaining strength, I stumbled out into the graveyard. Looking back over my shoulder, I saw Craig and the vampires appear in the open doorway. I raced away from them. Before I knew what had happened, someone had taken hold of me. Snapping my head round, I looked into the face of Potter. With a cigarette dangling from the corner of his mouth, he smiled and said, "What's the rush?"

I blinked. When I opened my eyes, I saw fleeting memories of cigarette ends lying beneath a tree next to the dead body of Henry Blake. Glimpses of Potter's mouth as he blew smoke from between his lips. Holding me tight, Potter grinned at me as if he knew what I was thinking.

Chapter Twenty

"Get off me!" I roared, throwing a punch at Potter. But with lightning speed, he snatched hold of my wrist and pulled my arm down by my side.

"That's no way to treat a friend and colleague," he said, blowing cigarette smoke into my face.

"You're no friend of mine," I spat. Trying to yank myself free of him, I could see he was in his police uniform and I thought how he wasn't fit to wear it.

"But *he's* your friend, right?" Potter asked, looking over my shoulder. I looked back to see Craig just outside the church door, twenty or so vampires standing behind him.

"I thought he was," I whispered to myself.

"Sergeant Phillips isn't your friend," someone said. I turned around to see Murphy. "And he certainly isn't a friend of ours."

Looking between the three of them, I said, "What's going on here?"

"Phillips went missing three years ago," Murphy said. "He used to be one of my constables."

"But that's impossible," I said. "He was my sergeant at training school."

"So that's where you've been hiding?" Murphy called out to Craig.

"Had someone looking after you, Phillips? Protecting you?" Potter said, over my shoulder.

Stepping away from the front of the church and coming towards us, Phillips smiled and said, "Not protecting, more like guiding me, showing me how things should be."

"So what did you do with her?" Murphy asked. "I mean, that's why you went missing, wasn't it?"

"Who are you talking about?" I asked them. I didn't mind who provided the answer, I just wanted to know what was going on.

"Your mother, Kiera," someone said from behind me, and glancing back over my shoulder, I watched as Luke stepped from the shadow of a large tree and into the swirling snow.

At the sight of him, my heart leapt, but I fought the urge to go to him. Out of everyone here, he was the one I wanted to trust. But could I? I remembered what Phillips had told me about him, how suspicion had fallen on him after my mother's disappearance.

"Phillips told me it was your fault my mother vanished," I shouted.

"I should've been there for her," Luke said coming towards me. "I was meant to have been crewed with her that night, but I was sent back beneath ground on a false errand. I now know it was your friend over there that sent me back," and he looked at Phillips. "When I realised I'd been tricked, I rushed back above ground, but I was too late. Phillips had vanished and taken your mother with him."

With my head spinning and not knowing who or what to believe, I looked at Craig and asked, "Is this

209

true?"

"Poor, beautiful Kiera," Craig smiled. "Can't you
see the truth for once?"

"Tell me!" I snapped.

"Your mother was the best," he said. "Her
ability to *see* was so superior to yours – you're almost
blind compared to her. She had me and what was going
on in this town all figured out within days of her arriving
and we couldn't let that be."

"Who's *we*?" I shouted.

There was the sound of thunder overhead and
we all looked up to see a winged figure falling like a
stone from the sky. Snow flurried all around it, making it
difficult to see who it was. The creature landed with a
thud, huge, black wings drawn around him like a cloak.
Then, as if shuddering, the wings unfurled to reveal
Rom. Stepping forward, Craig came to stand beside him,
and it was then I realised it was them I'd overheard in
the corridor at the police station earlier that night.
Pulling off his coat and tearing his shirt away, Craig
threw back his shoulders and as he did, his wings sprang
from his back.

Understanding how cruelly he'd tricked me and
had tried to lead me to my capture at the church, I
sprang forward, wanting to get at him. But Potter had
hold of my arm and yanked me back.

"Easy, tiger," he whispered in my ear. "All in
good time."

"Rom?" Murphy breathed, and he sounded
genuinely shocked and hurt. "So you are one of them?"

"If you mean by *them*, the Vampyrus that are sick and tired of living beneath the ground while the humans tread on us under foot, then yes, I'm one of *them*," Rom said, and his voice was calm but stern.

"But you've fed on humans. Look at the result of your actions!" Murphy said, pointing to the vampires that crowded behind Rom and Phillips. "Look what you've done!"

"You've broken the Vampyrus' rules of coming above ground," Luke said.

"Oh the *rules*," Rom said. "Stupid me."

"Why don't you join us?" Craig grinned. "You really don't know what you are missing."

"No thanks," Potter said, behind me. "I hate the sight of blood." And without having to look back at him, I knew he would have that wise guy smile of his spread across his face.

"You're pathetic, Potter," Rom almost seemed to growl. "You're all pathetic. How long do you think it will be before the humans invade The Hollows? Look at what they've done up here. Look at the chaos and devastation they've caused."

"And by feeding off them and turning them into some half-breed of us is making things better, is it?" Luke asked.

"For centuries there have been what the humans call 'vampires'," Rom said, as if justifying his actions. "Since the dawn of civilisation, Vampyrus have come above ground and fed, creating these vampires."

"And they've had to be hunted and destroyed,"

Murphy said. "Our history has proven that this is not the way. We have to find unity with the humans, find a way of living together."

"What, by sneaking around?" Phillips hissed. "Secretly living among them and scurrying back beneath ground every time you hunger for one of them? You're a disgrace to the Vampyrus if that's what you think. We should be able to fly and soar through the air. We should be *free*."

"And what about them?" Luke said, pointing at the vampires. "Are they free?"

"We've given them new life," Rom said. "They are better than they were before. They are like us."

"They're nothing like us," Murphy said. "They're mindless animals. Their only want and desire is to kill and destroy. We are better than that."

"Then join us," Rom spat. "Let us be the most powerful race on the planet."

"No thanks," Murphy hissed, unbuttoning his shirt.

Sensing that Murphy was readying himself to do battle, Rom and Phillips arched their wings high above them. "Give us Hudson and we will go," Rom said, as if suggesting a truce, using me as some kind of peace offering. "That's all we want. Let us have her."

"Never!" Luke roared, running towards them, tearing his shirt away in torn strips. Leaping into the air, his back twisted as his wings ripped through his flesh and fanned out on either side of him. I watched as he swooped upwards, racing towards Rom at a terrifying speed. In a blink, Rom shot from the ground and flew into the sky, clattering into Luke.

I looked at Murphy, who was now also stripped to the waist, and was neatly folding his police shirt in two.

"Don't you think you should go and help him or something?" I shouted.

"Okay, don't rush me," he grumbled. "I'm not as young as I used to be." For his age, like Rom, he was in pretty good shape. He wasn't exactly muscle bound, but he was toned. The only thing that gave his age away was the silver hairs that covered his chest. Placing his shirt on top of a nearby grave, he looked at me and said, "Make sure that doesn't get dirty."

Before I'd had a chance to say anything back, he was gone, his giant, bony, black wings propelling him through the night sky towards Luke and Rom. From behind me, I heard a roaring sound. Spinning around, I watched Potter spring into the air, and while airborne, he flung away his police jacket and shirt as his wings ripped out through his back. Within an instance, he was on Phillips. They spun and tumbled through the air as they grappled with one another.

There was a swooping sound above me and I looked up to see Rom plummeting through the sky. He had hold of something and whatever it was, it was thrashing about. As Rom whisked closer, I could see it was Murphy who was struggling with him. Then in a spray of shadows, I saw Luke appear as if from nowhere. There was another sound similar to that of thunder, and he spun through the air at Rom, his wings pinned back making him look like an eagle. Snatching hold of Rom's wings, he yanked him back and upwards into the sky. Rom lashed out with his fists, and in doing so, he dropped Murphy, who fell towards the ground. He dropped at such an incredible speed I feared he would smash straight into the gravestones beneath him. But within inches of hitting them, he spread his wings open like two black sails and soared upwards again.

Twisting around, I could see the vampires charging towards me. Stumbling backwards knowing I only had seconds to react, I grabbed two bottles of holy water from my coat pocket. Snatching off the lids, I held a bottle in each hand and squeezed. Jets of water shot from the ends of the bottles and straight into the faces of two approaching vampires.

They were running at me so fast that they didn't have time to stop or react. The holy water splashed off their faces, and at once they threw their claw-like hands over their eyes. The vampires screamed, and above their cries, I could hear the sound of hissing and spitting. The most disgusting thing I'd ever seen, happened. Their faces started to dribble through their fingers in thick, gloopy streams. One of them pulled its hands away, and I could see its left eye ooze from its socket and slide down its cheek.

"What have you done!" this one screeched.

"Have some more," I shouted, and emptied the bottle at him.

Within seconds his face, ears, and nose were

nothing more than a crimson red mess that was now sliding off its neck and down its chest. Clutching at the air, the vampire collapsed onto its knees, then went down completely.

Looking up, the second vampire still had its face covered with its hands. Taking my chance, I sprayed the last of the holy water at him. I could see the skin on his face bubbling and sizzling, and he pushed his hands against his head as if trying to hold it together. But within seconds it had collapsed inwards like melting putty. Staggering for just a moment, the vampire stumbled over and was still.

But there were more, and they leapt and bounded over the gravestones as they charged at me. Chucking the empty bottles away, I fumbled for two more.

"Come on!" I screamed, willing myself on.

"Hungry!" one of the vampires cried, pouncing off a nearby gravestone at me. With its arms outstretched, its long ivory nails slashed at my face. But then they were gone. I looked up to see the vampire cartwheeling through the air. My rescuer swooped in, and hovering just feet above me, Potter yelled, "Get out of here or you're gonna die, Kiera!" Then he was snatched away by Phillips as he swooped in and almost seemed to rugby tackle Potter in mid-air.

I raced across the graveyard, weaving myself amongst the gravestones. But the vampires were relentless, and once again started to hunt me down. I could hear their screeching and shrieking just feet away.

But I had taken a wrong turn and was now heading towards the back of the graveyard and the stone wall that reached up into the night.

With my heart racing, I started to panic.

"There must be a gate...a door...*anything*," I mumbled, but I knew I had nowhere to go. Looking back I could see several of the vampires striding towards me, their speed and agility terrifying. They were gaining on me with such speed I knew I wouldn't have time to get a crucifix or bottle from my pocket. They were within touching distance, so close the spit from their fangs spattered my face. I closed my eyes, then my stomach lurched and I felt the sensation of rising upwards off the ground. I opened my eyes, looked down. The church was just a pinprick below. Glancing upwards, expecting to see either Murphy or Potter but hoping for Luke, I screamed as Father Taylor grinned down at me.

Chapter Twenty-One

I was struck by how bony and repulsive the priest looked. His body was sickly white and sinewy-looking. The skin that held his bones together looked waxy and taut. The wings that arched from his back were black and leathery. They looked torn in places and the membrane was tattered and frayed. With his arms around me, he dragged me upwards through the freezing night air. Snow bombarded my face like ice cold pellets.

"What do you want from me?" I screamed over the howl of the wind.

"You're unique," he roared, his eyes, bright and knowing.

"How?" I yelled, as we swooped left and right.

"Like your mother!"

"Where is she?"

Father Taylor grinned, opened his mouth as if to answer, then screamed in anger. Before I'd realised what was happening, I was falling, rushing down through the night, my clothes rippling and my hair fluttering wildly. Spinning over and over, I caught a glimpse of what had caused the priest to release me. Murphy had dived in towards Taylor and punched through his wings. Losing control and altitude, the priest spiralled back towards the graveyard, his wings looking broken and limp.

Screaming, I fell behind him, the pressure of the wind crushing my chest. The church's steeple came into view and I raced towards it. With every second it got bigger and bigger until at the very last minute, I felt two powerful arms snaking around my waist. Looking around, I could see it was Luke who had me. Soaring away from the steeple, Luke smiled down into my face, his fangs gleaming.

"Okay?" he asked, holding me tight, making me feel safe at last.

"I've been better," I said, looking into his face. "I thought you'd been banished?"

"Not exactly," he said, banking right, sending my stomach into a series of somersaults. "We knew if I went away, it would flush Phillips out. He wouldn't have come for you with me hanging around."

"Why does everyone keep using me as bait?" I shouted over the wind.

"It must be those pretty eyes," he smiled back at me.

"So where did you go that night," I asked, "when I was calling for backup?"

"At the graveyard?"

"Yes."

"I saw Taylor fall on the way back to the church," he explained. "I was just about to go and help, when I saw Phillips step from the dark. Not believing it could be him, I went to take a closer look. Then I heard all hell breaking loose, so I came back to help and that's when I found you in the car wreck."

Pressing my face against his chest, I felt safe, and those intense feelings I'd experienced the night we had shared together came flooding back. My whole being seemed to tingle. I felt this sudden urge to tell him that I loved him, but why? I didn't even know him. He wasn't human. No one falls in love so quickly, especially not me. But deep down, in that place where you go at night – the place where you keep your innermost feelings – I was feeling something different. Something I couldn't remember ever feeling before.

Swooping to a sudden stop, Luke hovered by the branches of a tall tree. Lifting me gently into them, he said, "Stay here, you'll be safe."

"Don't leave me," I said.

"I'll be back for you." He kissed me. Easing himself away, Luke said, "I've got to go and help my friends. Wait for me." Then he was gone, corkscrewing up into the night, wings rippling in the wind.

"I've got nowhere to go," I breathed, watching him speed towards Murphy, who was soaring after Rom.

From the treetop, I saw Luke and Murphy race after Rom in a flicker of black shadows. They moved so fast through the sky, both Murphy and Luke seemed to blur out of existence. Looking ahead, I could see Potter and Phillips tumbling over and over through the air as they fought with each other. Holding my breath, I watched as they plummeted towards the church roof, then through it. Roof slates and chunks of masonry and stone exploded up into the night. Within seconds, the door of the church burst outwards in a spray of splinters as Phillips came crashing through it and into a nearby gravestone, which cracked in half under the force of him colliding into it.

Potter appeared in the church doorway, and wasting no time, he launched himself at Phillips who lay momentarily stunned in the snow. Just as he was about to get up, Potter was on him, his wings shimmering in the candlelight shining from within the church. Potter thrust his head forward and I could hear his teeth tearing and biting at Phillips who lay screaming beneath him. Potter's attack was frenzied, black jets of blood pumping from wounds on Phillips' face and neck. The snow all around them started to turn crimson and I looked away. Even though Phillips had lied to me and had something to do with my mother's disappearance, I still didn't want to watch him die, being ripped to shreds in a bleak, barren graveyard.

From my hiding place, I saw the remaining vampires, speeding amongst the gravestones towards Potter who had his back turned to them. Knowing they were only seconds from him, I screamed, "Potter! Get out of there!"

Potter drew away from Phillips and looked up, the lower half of his face dripping with blood. Seeing the approaching vampires, he sprang into the air, leaving Phillips lying lifeless in a crimson mound of snow. Potter looped in the air, and then came racing back towards the vampires. But like Potter, some of the vampires had heard my scream from high up in the tree and this had drawn their attention to me. Splitting, three of them raced towards the foot of the tree and started scrambling up the trunk. They climbed like spiders, the sound of their long fingernails scratching against the rough bark. Within seconds they were clawing their way over the snow-laden branches and scuttling towards me. Reaching into my pocket for the crucifixes and bottles of holy water, I nearly fell from the tree when I realised that they were gone.

"Where are they?" I cried.

I patted both pockets to make sure, but they were empty. Realising they must have fallen out while falling through the sky, I frantically backed away up the branch from the approaching vampires.

Hissing and spitting, they came forward, their eyes glowing red and orange. Leaning back, I kicked out at one of them.

"Get the fuck off me!" I screamed.

The heel of my boot smashed into the jaw of the lead vampire. There was a cracking sound as his jaw broke, jutting out at an odd angle. With a crooked smile, he snapped his jaw back into place.

"Is that the best you can do?" he screeched, continuing forward, sniffing the air like an animal on the scent of its prey.

With nowhere left to go, I prayed that perhaps one of the Vampyrus would come and save me. But as I said my silent prayer, I heard the roar of Luke's and Murphy's wings as they screamed past me in pursuit of Rom. I glanced down, and through the branches of the tree, I could see that Potter was enthusiastically ripping to pieces the vampires that had gone after him.

Knowing that if I were to survive, it would be down to my own wits and courage, I had an idea. Reaching out, I ripped two solid-looking branches away from the trunk. Both were about twelve inches in length and were splintered and ragged at each end. Placing one over the other, I made a cross. Holding it out, I waved the makeshift crucifix desperately in front of the vampire's face. It recoiled as if in fear, its lips rolling back and revealing its fangs.

"It works," I whispered with relief.

Then the vampire looked at me and gave a knowing smile as if it had been tricking me all along. "It hasn't been blessed," the vampire spat, lunging at me.

Recoiling in horror, I pulled my arms against my chest to protect myself, the branches jutting out from my hands. The vampire landed on top of me, its teeth snapping inches from my neck, its breath hot against my flesh. It jerked violently against me.

"No!" it spat, and lurched back away from me, the glow in its dead eyes fading. Looking down, I saw one of the branches I'd been holding, protruding from a bloody hole in its chest. The vampire looked down at the jagged piece of wood sticking from it. Sensing its fear and revulsion at the sight of the makeshift stake, I dared to lean forward, and gripping the branch, I drove it further into the vampire's heart.

"Away!" it screamed, clutching frantically at the branch with its claws.

"Just die!" I screeched, twisting the piece of wood deeper into the pumping red wound. Almost at once, its claws began to turn grey, then crumble like the ash on the tip of one of Potter's cigarettes. The vampire's fingers seemed to snap and break, the wind snatching them away in small, broken particles.

Looking down at its dissolving fingers, the vampire howled, "Look what you've done to me!"

Reaching out, I thrust the branch with the heel of my hand, so far into its heart, that the piece of wood disappeared.

Just like its hands, its face began to crumble away, like smashed plaster. First its jaw went and its swollen, black tongue rolled down onto its chest. It made a disgusting flopping sound and I turned away. Covering my face with my hands, I peeked through the fingers that still held the second branch. Within moments the vampire had disintegrated into a pile of smoking ash that swirled away on the snow.

Undeterred, the second vampire came forward, scuttling along the branch towards me. I brandished the ragged piece of wood at it and screamed, "Come on then!"

Crazed by its lust for blood, it leapt through the air at me. Steadying myself against a fork in the branches, I rammed the makeshift stake into its chest. Shrieking in pain, it shot backwards out of the tree, its claws clutching at the air. As it fell, it hooked its ivory-coloured fingernails into the hem of my jeans and dragged me out of the tree with it.

"Please don't let me die!" I screamed, wrapping my arms around a branch, and clenching my teeth. Looking down, I could see the vampire swinging from my leg.

"LET...GO...OF...ME!" I screeched. And in between each word, I kicked out, desperate to shake the vampire loose. It wailed in agony, and with its free hand it tried to pull the stake from its chest. But as it did, the vampire's fingers started to fall to pieces in little powdery chunks.

Bit by bit, the vampire slowly began to disintegrate like a sandcastle being swallowed up by a wave. The hand that was holding onto my leg separated from the vampire's wrist and it fell from the tree, smashing into a powdery mess against a gravestone below. Kicking out my leg, I shook the vampire's hand free and it blew away.

"Thank you, God," I breathed.

Hoisting myself back up into the tree, the third vampire came scuttling towards me through the branches. But my heart ached and tears welled in my eyes, when I saw it was Henry Blake looking back at me. His tiny, broken body, neck, and torso ripped apart.

"Henry," I whispered.

Ignoring me, he advanced, his eyes burning red, lips twisted up into a snarl baring his pointed teeth.

"Please, Henry," I whispered again. I just couldn't bring myself to destroy him. Still he came forward, and I knew in my heart that he wouldn't show me the same compassion I wanted to show him.

He was then upon me, knocking me back into the branches of the tree where I became entangled. I twisted beneath him, trying to keep my neck and face away from his lunging bites.

"No, Henry!" I screamed, but he was deaf to me.

Then he was gone, flying backwards through the branches, his tiny, broken, hands snatching for anything to take hold of. He seemed to dangle in the air. Potter came into view. He was holding the kicking, spitting boy out at arm's length.

"Going soft, Constable Hudson?" he said in his cocky manner.

"He's just a child," I said back.

"He's a monster," Potter said, this time his voice was low and serious.

"I can't watch," I told him.

"Don't then," he said.

I looked away, and even though I covered my ears, I could still hear the screams of the boy – the monster – as Potter ended it for him.

"Are you coming or are you going to play around in this tree all night?" I heard Potter say once he'd finished with the boy.

Looking back over my shoulder, I could see Potter hovering on the other side of the tree branches. His wings flapped steadily up and down, his arms down by his sides, his stomach muscles taut.

Shame about the personality, I thought to myself as I looked at his muscular body. Placing one hand over the next, I climbed towards him. Lifting me into his arms, he held me close as we raced back towards the ground. Potter was travelling so fast that it didn't seem like he'd given us enough time to stop and land safely.

"Slow down!" I shouted, my heart in my throat as the ground raced up to meet us.

Opening his giant, black wings, we slowed and landed as gently as a feather upon the ground. Seeing that he had shaken me, Potter smiled and said, "There's no need to get excited."

Pulling myself free of his grasp, I looked at him and said, "I can promise you, Potter, that there is nothing you could ever do that would excite me."

Smiling, Potter lit a cigarette. He winked at me and said, "Well, see about that."

Then he was gone, soaring back up into the sky. I watched him go as he headed towards Luke and Murphy, who were struggling with Rom.

From behind me, there was a noise. Spinning round expecting more vampires to be rushing me, I saw Father Taylor come limping from the shadows of the church. The tips of his battered wings were trailing in the snow. Crouching down behind a gravestone, I watched him approach Phillips' broken, bleeding body. Kneeling beside him, he leant over and seemed to study his friend's injuries.

Part of me wanted to step from my hiding place and ask him what he meant when he had told me I was 'unique'. But more than that, I wanted to ask him what had happened to my mother. But before I'd the chance to muster up the courage, there was the sound of beating wings above me. Looking over my shoulder, I could see Luke, Murphy, and Potter dragging Rom between them from the sky. Taylor must have heard them too, because as I looked back, he had lifted Phillips into his arms, then with a struggle, he flapped his wings in a series of jerky movements and flew away into the night.

Stepping out from behind the grave, I approached the others who now had Rom captured between them. He struggled, but it was pointless. Looking at them he said, "Just get it over with, but know, there are others like me."

"Who?" Luke snapped.

Rom just smiled at him. Coming closer, Murphy saw me and said, "Kiera, go away, this has nothing to do with you."

"It has everything to do with me," I told him. "He knows what happened to my mother." Then going toe to toe with Rom, I looked into his eyes and said, "Where is she?"

Looking back at me, Rom smiled and said, "If you can't *see* her, then I'm real sorry about that."

"What do you mean?" I asked.

"Look and you will *see,* Kiera. But be careful of what you *look* for, you might not like what you *find!*" he said, lowering his head, resolute to his fate.

I knew he would say nothing more. It was as if his final pleasure would be to torment me. Taking me by the shoulders, Luke looked deeply into my eyes and said, "Kiera, you don't need to see this."

"But -" I started.

"He can't be changed or cured," Luke said. Turning away from me, he spread his wings, along with Murphy and Potter, to shield me from what they were about to do. But I could still hear the sound of biting, ripping, and tearing.

Chapter Twenty-Two

"Is that the last of them?" Murphy asked, and I watched him wipe Rom's blood from his chin with his forearm.

Still turned away from Rom's remains, I couldn't bring myself to look, Potter strode forward and said, "Phillips' body is over there."

"It's not," I told him. Potter looked at me, running his tongue over his lips, mopping up the red gunge that was there. "I saw Taylor fly away with the body," I told him.

Luke came towards me, but didn't make eye contact, and I wondered if he thought I was repulsed by him for what he had just done. In a way I was, but I understood the reasons why. Rom and the others weren't like Luke, Murphy, and Potter, and if they hadn't been destroyed, then they would've only continued to feed off humans and create more vampires. So understanding his shame, I went to him and took his hand in mine.

"This isn't good," Murphy said, picking up his shirt. "We should've destroyed them all."

"Do you want me to go after Taylor?" Potter asked, lighting another cigarette.

"No," Murphy said, arching his back, which made an audible cracking noise. His wings shrunk back beneath his flesh and he pulled on his shirt. "It will be dawn soon and we need to get rid of any remains. We also need to make sure all of those vampires have been destroyed."

Pulling a cigarette lighter from his pocket, Potter flipped it on. Waving the flame in front of his face, he looked at Murphy and said, "The usual way?"

Nodding, Murphy buttoned up the front of his shirt and put on his police jacket. He looked at Luke, and said, "Take Kiera back to the Inn and get back here as quickly as possible and give us a hand in sorting this mess out."

"But I want to stay," I said.

"No," Murphy insisted.

"But -" I started.

"Constable Hudson, despite everything that has happened, I'm still your sergeant," he growled," and I'm telling you to get out of here."

Before I'd the chance to say anything back, Luke had wrapped his arms around my waist and I felt myself soaring upwards. Looking down, I could just make out the outlines of Murphy and Potter as they walked towards the church. Then they were gone, hidden by a cloud. With the wind whistling through my hair and Luke's wings beating slowly up and down, we rose over The Ragged Cove. To be so high above the town felt tranquil and my shredded nerves started to soften. Luke pulled me close and it felt as if I were being carried away by an angel. Circling around in the sky, we soared through the clouds and began to lose altitude. From above, I could see the town stretched out before me and it looked peaceful and somehow beautiful with its ragged coast line, white beaches, and miles of woodland. Looking down at it, it was hard to believe the tiny town had hidden such nightmares. Then, in the distance, like a giant torch, I saw St. Mary's steeple raging with fire.

Landing a short distance from the Inn, Luke uncurled his wings from around me, but didn't let go.

"Are you okay?" he asked, his voice soft and caring.

"I'll be fine," I told him, looking up into those bright green eyes. Holding me against him, he brushed his cheek against mine, and I could feel the tingle of his black stubble.

"I'll come back," he whispered in my ear.

"You'd better," I whispered.

"Tonight," he said. "Once we've taken care of everything back at the church."

"What about the others?" I asked.

"The others?" he asked, looking down at me.

"Rom said there were others just like him," I reminded Luke.

"Later," he said. "Murphy will know what to do."

"Come back then," I said, not wanting to let go.

"In a flash," he smiled, and then pulling me close again, he kissed me. But this time it was different. His previous kisses had been soft, but these were urgent and had a passion I could only describe as bordering on hunger. Kissing him back, I matched his intensity and a

231

wave of deep desire washed over me. Not wanting to break the spell, but not wanting to lose myself either, I pulled gently away from him. Staring up at him, I said, "Later."

Smiling, Luke arched his back, and spreading his jet-black wings, he was gone. Turning towards the Inn, I heard the sound of a thunderclap way off in the distance.

Roland was behind the bar and was drying some beer glasses with a filthy-looking towel. Seeing me step in through the door, he rushed over.

"Kiera, you look awful," he said, sounding concerned.

"Thanks," I half-smiled.

With his pink-coloured jowls flushing red, he said, "I didn't mean it like that." Then looking me up and down and noticing the dried vampire blood on my clothes, hands, and face, he added, "You look like you've been to hell and back, my poor dear."

"You don't know how close to the truth you are," I told him, feeling the first aches and pains of my adventure.

"Why don't you go and freshen-up?" he smiled. "I'll bring you up a nice warm mug of cocoa and something to eat. You look half starved."

I could see the willingness to please in his eyes and I didn't have it in my heart to knock back his kind offer again. So smiling back at him, I said, "That would be really sweet of you, Roland. Thank you."

I watched him rush back to the kitchen, and then I made my way up to my room. Wincing, I pulled off my clothes. I looked at my body and was shocked to see how many cuts and bruises covered it. Pulling on my bathrobe, I ran myself a bath. While I waited for it to fill up, I went and lay on my bed. Listening to the water splash and tumble into the bath, I closed my eyes. I thought of Luke returning later and a wave of nervous excitement covered me from head to foot. With my skin tingling at the thought of him touching me, I tried to push him from my mind. The feelings I sometimes had for him scared me, but I think that's what I secretly liked – the fact that he could make me feel this way.

Remembering the events of that night, my mind kept returning to what Taylor had said. What had he meant when he told me I was unique? We're all unique aren't we? But I knew he had meant something more than that. Then the voice of Rom entered my head as he told me I could look for my mother but I might not like what I *see*. Those images of the hairs in Henry Blake's dead little hand swam back before me, followed by pictures of the hairs I'd discovered caught in the teeth of the hairbrush I found in my locker – the locker I guessed had once been used by 'Jessica Reeves' – my mother. Had she really been at that crime scene? I'd accounted for everyone else who had been there. Taylor, Phillips, and the smoker. But who had that been? Not Potter as I'd thought, so who then?

The sound of tapping at my door dragged me from my thoughts. Pulling my bathrobe tight about me,

I went and opened it. Roland stood on the other side, and I could hear his chest wheezing from his climb up the stairs. In his chubby hands he carried a silver tray. On it there was a steaming hot mug of cocoa and a plate of neatly cut sandwiches. Stepping aside, I waved Roland into my room.

"You're very kind," I said to him as he placed the tray on the desk.

"It's no bother at all," he said, turning around and looking at me. I noticed his eyes wander down, and following his gaze, I could see that my bathrobe had come open slightly, revealing my right leg up to the thigh. Feeling uncomfortable, I pulled the robe closed.

Sensing my discomfort, and without looking back at me, Roland shuffled towards the door and said, "Goodnight, Kiera."

"Goodnight, Roland," I said, closing the door behind him.

Crossing back to the table, I took a sip of the cocoa, and it tasted warm and sweet. Taking it with me into the bathroom, I turned off the taps. Fixing my hair into a bun at the base of my neck, I went back to my room and shrieked with surprise. Roland was back in my room, standing with his back against the closed door.

"What are you doing here?" I asked, gooseflesh crawling all over me.

"I just want to talk," he said, looking at me.

Pulling my bathrobe tight again, I said, "I really don't have time now Roland, I'm expecting a friend any minute."

Stepping away from the door and coming towards me, he said, "What I have to say won't take long."

Backing away from him, I said, "Please, Roland, if you wouldn't mind saving this for tomorrow."

"What I have to say can't wait until tomorrow," he said, unbuttoning his shirt.

Realising I was in serious trouble, I clenched my fists and shouted at him, "Roland, will you please leave my room!"

Pulling off his shirt and dropping it to the floor, he didn't take his eyes off me for a moment. His huge stomach was white, which made the wiry black hairs that covered it stand out even more than they should have. Once free of his shirt, his belly hung down over the top of his trousers like a mountain of white dough. Backing away towards the bathroom door, I looked for anything I could use as a weapon against him. Glancing down at the floor, I could see that something had fallen from his shirt pocket as he had disregarded it. Screwing up my eyes, I could see it was a pack of Marlboro cigarettes. Almost at once I saw the base of the tree in the woods next to the body of the Blake boy. I saw glimpses of those cigarette butts left by the killer who had waited for the others in the woods.

As if to prove my *visions* and instincts right, Roland threw his head back and wailed like an animal in pain. I looked at him. Roland's whole body wobbled, as two black wings grew from his back. Unlike the other Vampyrus wings I'd seen, Roland's were covered in a coat of greasy, black hair. They glistened in the light from the desk lamp. Rolling his head forward, he looked at me, and I could see that where he had once had a neat row of stained, yellow teeth, he now had a set of discoloured fangs.

"Surprised, are you?" he asked, his voice low, like a growl.

"Luke will be here anytime now," I threatened him.

"Bishop doesn't scare me," he leered.

"Murphy and Potter will be with him," I said, trying anything to get him to flee.

Holding his belly with both of his meaty hands, he released a throaty chuckle. "Oh please, Kiera, you're really scaring me now."

"You should be scared," I told him, my voice wavering. "I saw what they did to Rom tonight."

"Rom?" he laughed again. "Rom was nothing compared to those that come next. We were sent just to pave the way."

"We?" I asked, now backed into the bathroom with nowhere to run or hide.

"Rom, Taylor, Phillips, and me," he smiled. "We are just mere disciples."

"For who?" I said.

"Roland!" a voice shouted from behind him.

He turned, and looking past him, I could see his mother standing in the doorway of my room. Her wrinkled-looking face and eyes seething with anger.

"Mother, this has nothing to do with you!" he

barked at her.

"Enough, Roland!" she screeched back. "Haven't you done enough damage?"

"It's only just starting," he said, turning back towards me.

Roland grabbed for me, and as he did, he was yanked sharply backwards, crashing into the wall on the opposite side of the room. Believing Luke had arrived, my heart leapt and I raced from the bathroom and into the bedroom. But he wasn't there, just the old woman and her son.

Getting up from the floor and flapping his wings in anger, he leapt towards his mother, landing inches from her. "Mother, go back downstairs and do whatever it is you do and leave this to me!"

Making her short height count, the old woman straightened her curved back and confronted her son. "For too long I've covered for you, Roland," she said. "For too long I've sat back and watched you murder the innocent people of this town to satisfy your lust for their blood. But no more Roland – it ends tonight."

"I won't tell you again, mother," Roland shouted. "Now go back downstairs and mind your own business!"

"It *is* my business!" she spat. "We could've had a good life above ground. We had something good going here. But instead of going back under when the hunger was upon you, you gave into it. You're weak, pathetic, and I'm so ashamed of you."

'Mother…" he started.

"No, Roland!" she screeched." I'm sick and tired of having to try and protect the good people of this town from the vampires you've created, and from you. For years now I've pushed those bottles of holy water and crucifixes onto the people of this town in the hope that it might protect them. But I'm tired of it, Roland. Please stop. If not for yourself, do it for me."

He looked into his mother's eyes and for a moment, I hoped what she said to him had made some impact. Snarling, he said to her, "And you say I'm pathetic." Knocking her to the floor, he turned towards me again. But before he had taken one step in my direction, his mother sprung into the air, a faded set of black wings flapping behind her. Reaching for him, she clawed at his back and pulled him down. Roland rolled over, crushing his wings. The old woman lunged at him, but drawing his knees into his chest, he kicked out, sending her spinning across the room. She crashed into the wall, which shuddered and then cracked, brick dust showering the room. She hit the floor with a sickening thud, and I thought she must be dead or at least have broken all the bones in her body. But no sooner had she hit the floor, she was up again, racing towards her son. Screeching, she clawed at his face, and he covered his head with his large hands.

"Get off me, mother!" Roland roared.

"No more!" she screamed.

Flitting all around him, her delicate and fragile-looking wings humming up and down, she struck out at him, a diagonal gash appearing across his face. Wiping the blood away with the back of his hand, his eyes shone black with hate for her. Launching himself from the floor, he smashed into her, sending her spinning across the room. Again she crashed into the wall, lumps of plaster spraying up from all around her. But this time, she looked dazed and stunned. Seizing his chance, he was upon her. Taking her head in his bulky hands, he twisted it sharply to the right.

"Sorry, mother," he said, which was followed by a cracking sound. She fell limp in his arms, her neck broken as easily as a stick of chalk.

Letting her drop to the floor as if she had meant nothing to him, Roland got up. Turning to face me he smiled, and said, "Where were we? Oh yes, I remember," and he threw himself at me. Crashing to the floor, Roland sat on top of me, his colossal weight, squeezing the air from my lungs.

"Don't kill me," I gasped, looking into his bloated face.

"I don't want to kill you, Kiera," he said. "You're far too precious for that."

"What do you mean?" I croaked.

"You really have no idea, do you?" he said. "Didn't your mother tell you anything?"

"About what?" I mumbled beneath him, the last of the air leaving my lungs. Everything around me started to turn black and I fought to stay conscious. Just as I was about to pass out, the bedroom window exploded inwards in a shower of broken glass. I looked up in time to see Luke perched on the window ledge like a giant bird of prey.

"Get off her," Luke said, and I had never heard such anger in his voice before.

Glancing back over his shoulder, Roland said, "If I were you, I'd disappear back into The Hollows, boy. After all, that's what you're best at."

Without asking him a second time, Luke reached out with one hand, gripped the back of Roland's neck, and tossed him across the room as if he were nothing more than a paper kite. At once, I could breathe again and I sucked in deep lungful's of air. Sitting up, I watched Roland crash through the wall that separated the bedroom and the bathroom. The wall crumpled into a pile of brick and plaster onto the threadbare carpet, and the ceiling above it sagged inwards as if it was going to collapse. Within seconds, Roland had sprung back into the room, brandishing his teeth.

Leaping from the window ledge, Luke snarled back and slammed into Roland. They locked arms, and threw each other back and forth across the room. Like wild animals, they snapped at one other, their fangs ripping and tearing at each other's flesh. Scrambling out of their way, I huddled myself into the far corner of the room. Roland ducked under Luke's arm as he swung for him. Then with both hands, he thrust out at Luke, sending him crashing through the doorway into the hall outside. The door came away from its frame in an explosion of jagged splinters. Brushing himself off, Luke got up and raced back into the room. Jumping into the air, he shoulder-barged into Roland's chest, lifting him off his feet and sending him smashing through the window from which he had come. Pouncing onto the window ledge, Luke peered out into the dark.

Scrambling from the corner, I ran towards Luke. "Can you see him?" I asked.

Without answering me, Luke curled his arm around my waist and said, "Hold tight!"

Within moments, we were high above The Ragged Cove again, the howling wind and swirling snow all around us. Wrapping my bathrobe around me, I wished I'd had time to change. I looked at Luke's face and it was a mask of grim determination as we flew upwards. Looking down, I saw Roland racing after us, his wings folded by his sides to give him greater propulsion.

"He's right behind us!" I shouted.

Tucking me beneath him, and arching his wings, Luke thrust forward. And then that sound came again – the thunderclap – which I'd heard so often before.

"What is that noise?" I asked, terrified of its deafening rumble and the vibrations it sent through me.

"It's a sonic boom," he shouted back.

A sonic boom? I asked myself. Could we really be travelling so fast?

Banking hard to the right, I clung to Luke, my arms and legs wrapped around him, as we dived away from Roland and out to sea. Then plummeting down, we rushed towards the black, heaving waves of the ocean. Racing just feet from its surface, sea water sprayed out behind us like the waves caused by a speedboat, soaking my bathrobe and hair. Glancing back over my shoulder, I could see that Roland was just feet away from us. He snatched at the air, trying to take hold of me, but Luke twisted and rolled to the left and headed back towards land. Within seconds, jagged cliff faces were sweeping towards us. Believing we didn't have enough time to change direction, I closed my eyes and clenched my teeth, readying myself for the impact. But it never came. Opening my eyes, I could see the jagged cliff face as we soared vertically up it.

Swooping over the top of the cliff, I could see the burning steeple of St. Mary's in the distance. It was at least three or four miles away. We reached it within seconds. Darting into the smoke, we came to a sudden stop. The smoke was thick and dark. I couldn't see more than a foot or two ahead of me. It was hot and choking. It filled my nose and made my eyes sting and water.

"Why have we stopped?" I sputtered.

"Shhh!" Luke hissed, looking quickly from left to right. "Here he comes," he said.

Roland appeared in the smoke ahead of us, and he just seemed to hover.

"Give me the girl," he said, "and this will all be over."

"You want her?" Luke roared. "Come and get her!" Then he let go of me.

Screaming, I dropped like a deadweight through the blistering hot smoke. "Luke!" I cried, unable to believe he had let go of me. Looking down, I could see the seething flames of the burning steeple racing towards me. Glancing up one last time in the hope it had been a mistake and I would see Luke coming to my rescue, all I saw was the gleaming yellow fangs of Roland as he lunged for me. Hoping the flames would take me before he did; I closed my eyes and felt myself being suddenly yanked sideways, away from the fire. Snapping open my eyes, I was staring into the face of Luke. He kissed me, and then threw me away like a rag doll.

"Catch her!" he roared, as Potter appeared from nowhere and caught hold of me.

Glancing back, I briefly saw the look of horror on Roland's face as he realised how he had been tricked. Having me snatched from his clutches at the very last moment, he had no time to slow his descent and he shot into the seething flames like a bullet. But to my horror, he grabbed hold of Luke and pulled him down into the raging inferno with him.

"No!" I screamed, kicking against Potter.

Holding me tight, Potter plunged towards the graveyard. Setting me down, I looked at him and shouted, "You've got to save Luke!" But he didn't seem to be listening to me. Instead he was looking up at the top of the burning steeple. With tears flowing down my cheeks, I followed his stare to see Roland shoot from the flames high above us. His wings glowed orange with fire and he spun over and over in the air as the flames consumed him. From the ground, I could hear his agonising shrieks, as he fought to put himself out. He fluttered left and right, until he finally fell still and dropped out of the sky like a blazing meteorite.

Pulling my robe tight against the freezing cold, I took hold of Potter's arm and shook it. I looked into his eyes and pleaded with him. "You've got to save Luke. He's in there!"

Looking back at me, Potter said, "For someone who doesn't get excited, you're doing a pretty good impression."

Stunned by what he'd said, I shook him again and screamed, "That's your friend in there!"

Popping a cigarette between his lips, he smiled at me and said, "Easy, tiger, we've got everything under control."

"Who's *we*?" I asked as Potter pointed over my shoulder. Spinning round, I saw Murphy sweep from the burning doorway of the church, carrying Luke in his arms. Racing towards me, Murphy landed and gently laid Luke in the snow at my feet. His wings were folded over him like a blanket. Tendrils of smoke rose from them as they smouldered.

"Will he be okay?" I asked Murphy.

"I don't know," he said, staring down at his friend. "I was in there as soon as I saw him fall into the flames. But the smoke and heat were so intense. It was hard to see him."

Kneeling down, I gently peeled back the edge of Luke's wings so I could look at him. His face was black with smoke and soot. I brushed his thick hair from his brow and kissed him.

"Wake up!" I whispered.

Nothing.

"Please, Luke," I cried. "You can't stand me up like this. We were meant to be having a date tonight, remember? I'm out here in the cold with nothing on except my bathrobe, my hair's a mess, and my feet are freezing. Just take me home so I can get ready, okay?"

Nothing.

Looking up at Murphy and Potter, I pleaded with them, "Don't just stand there, do *something!*" And for just the briefest of moments, I was sure I saw a flicker of concern in Potter's eyes.

"There's nothing we can do," Murphy said, squeezing my shoulder with his hand.

Knocking it away not wanting to be comforted by him, I leant over Luke and hugged him, my body shuddering with grief. Planting the softest of kisses on his perfect mouth, I whispered, "I'm going to miss you."

"I know," Luke whispered back, the faintest of smiles tugging at his lips.

Chapter Twenty-Three

We never did get to spend that night together. Luke was seriously injured and close to death. Murphy said he would only heal if Luke were taken back down into The Hollows. So carrying him in his arms, Murphy flew him back to the station. Potter took me, and for once, there were no wisecracks or cocky remarks. Stopping to collect my belongings from the Inn, Potter was silent, almost sombre. While I changed out of my bathrobe and into some warm clothes, Potter took the body of the old woman and placed her in the fire that was still raging at St. Mary's church.

By the time Potter had returned, I'd gathered together all of my belongings and it was like I'd never been there. Swooping up into the night, Potter raced us back to the station.

Luke had been laid on a cot in one of the cells, and I found Murphy leaning over him.

"Is he okay?" I asked, stepping into the cell.

"For now," he said, turning to look at me. "But we need to get him underground soon."

Moving towards the cot, I knelt down beside it. Luke was pale all over, blisters covered his face, and it looked raw in places. His wings had folded away, and he lay with his hands across his chest. I felt a hand on my shoulder and I looked up. "I'll leave you with him, while Potter and I clear this place out," Murphy said.

"What do you mean?" I asked. "Are you all going back?"

"Our work is done here," he said. "It's time we moved on. Taylor and Phillips, if still alive, are dangerous. They will go someplace else, another town or city and start all over."

"But -" I started.

"There can be no buts, Kiera. We have to go after them. Taylor and any others who join him can't be reasoned with and they can't be cured now that they've fed off humans. Like Rom, the only way of putting an end to this is...well, you know the rest," he said, turning away. At the door, he stopped and said, "You've got five minutes to say your goodbyes." Then he was gone, shouting orders at Potter to destroy any evidence they had ever been at the station.

Turning to Luke, I stroked his hair from his brow. With a flutter of his eyelids, he opened his eyes and looked at me. He half-smiled and said my name.

"Shhh," I told him.

"Kiera," he said again. "I've got to go back," he whispered.

"I know," I told him. "I'll wait here for you."

Momentarily closing his eyes in pain, he opened them again and said, "I won't be coming back here. When I'm better, I'll be going with Murphy and Potter to track down the others."

"Where will you go?" I asked him, a sudden sense of regret that I might never see him again.

"Wherever they go, so will we, until it's over,"

he whispered. "I don't know how long that will take or where it will lead. Come with us. You're a great investigator and you can *see* things we can't. You could help us."

All of my instincts urged me to agree – to say yes. Not to help hunt Taylor and Phillips, but so I could be with Luke. Leaning in close and kissing him on the mouth, I whispered, "No."

"No?" he said, looking confused.

"However much I want to come with you, Luke, I can't," I told him, my heart aching as I said those words.

"Why?"

"I have a promise to keep," I said, thinking of my father.

"To whom?" he asked, closing his eyes again.

"It doesn't matter," I said. Then picturing Henry Blake's tiny, dead hand clutching those hairs, I added, "I need to find my mother."

"But she could be dead," Luke said, his eyes still closed as if trying to control the pain he was in.

"I don't think she is," I told him.

"But how can you be sure?"

"It was something I *saw*," I whispered.

Murphy appeared in the cell doorway. "It's time," he said, coming over and scooping Luke up into his arms. He carried him out into the corridor and I followed. The hatch was open, and the filing cabinets, lockers, and desk drawers lay open and empty.

"Where's Potter?" I asked.

"He had to do one last thing before he could leave," Murphy said, glancing back over his shoulder at me. Then laying Luke on the floor by the open grate, he looked at me and said, "Take good care of yourself, Constable Hudson. It's been a pleasure working with you." Taking me by surprise, he threw his arms around me and held me tight. I hugged him back.

"None of you are real cops, are you?" I asked him.

"Not the way you think," he whispered in my ear. "But in The Hollows we are — kind of. We want to stop the bad guys just like you do."

Letting go of me, he pulled his pipe from his back pocket and popped the end of it between his lips. Then patting down his pockets in search of his matches, he said, "Where has Potter got to? We should be gone already."

"Stop panicking, sarge," someone said, and I looked up to see Potter coming down the corridor from the direction of the police station door. Shaking snow from his hair and bare shoulders, he shuddered, but not with the cold, it was his wings folding away.

Murphy climbed into the hole. Holding out his hands, he said to Potter, "Pass Luke down to me."

I watched as Potter scooped Luke up and lowered him into the hole. With my heart feeling like it was being crushed in my chest, Luke opened his eyes and looked back at me. "I love you," he said.

"I know," I smiled, and he was gone.

Potter climbed into the hole.

"What about me?" I said.

"What about you?" he asked, looking back at me.

"How do I get out of this town? The phones don't work, my car is stuck up that road and -"

Cutting over me, Potter said, "That's your problem, Hudson. You figure it out." Pulling the grate closed over him, he swung it shut. Then poking his hand up through the grating, he locked it with the padlock, taking the key with him.

Standing over the grate and looking down, I could hear a rumbling sound as the walls of the tunnel collapsed, hiding any evidence it had ever been there.

Turning away, I walked back into the office, picking up knocked-over chairs and straightening disarranged cabinets and drawers. With no idea as to what to do next, I knew that until the weather changed, I was trapped in The Ragged Cove. Crossing to the window, I looked up into the dawn sky and to my relief I could see that the snow had stopped falling at last. Then I saw something that raised my hopes even more. Rushing from the police station, I went to my battered old Mini which now sat by the curb. *Who had brought it here for me?* I wondered. Spying a folded piece of paper tucked beneath one of the wipers, I reached for it. Pulling it free, I unfolded the piece of paper and read what had been scribbled on it.

You really need to get yourself a new car – this is a piece of junk! Potter

Smiling to myself, I screwed up the piece of paper and went back into the station, locking the door behind me.

Vampire Wake

(Kiera Hudson Series One) Book 2

Available Now

More books by Tim O'Rourke

Kiera Hudson Series One

Vampire Shift (Kiera Hudson Series 1) Book 1

Vampire Wake (Kiera Hudson Series 1) Book 2

Vampire Hunt (Kiera Hudson Series 1) Book 3

Vampire Breed (Kiera Hudson Series 1) Book 4

Wolf House (Kiera Hudson Series 1) Book 5

Vampire Hollows (Kiera Hudson Series 1) Book 6

Kiera Hudson Series Two

Dead Flesh (Kiera Hudson Series 2) Book 1

Dead Night (Kiera Hudson Series 2) Book 2

Dead Angels (Kiera Hudson Series 2) Book 3

Dead Statues (Kiera Hudson Series 2) Book 4

Dead Seth (Kiera Hudson Series 2) Book 5

Dead Wolf (Kiera Hudson Series 2) Book 6

Dead Water (Kiera Hudson Series 2) Book 7

Dead Push (Kiera Hudson Series 2) Book 8

Dead Lost (Kiera Hudson Series 2) Book 9

Dead End (Kiera Hudson Series 2) Book 10

Kiera Hudson Series Three

The Creeping Men (Kiera Hudson Series Three) Book 1

The Lethal Infected (Kiera Hudson Series Three) Book 2

The Adoring Artist (Kiera Hudson Series Three) Book 3

The Secret Identity (Kiera Hudson Series Three) Book 4

Werewolves of Shade

Werewolves of Shade (Part One)

Werewolves of Shade (Part Two)

Werewolves of Shade (Part Three)

Werewolves of Shade (Part Four)

Werewolves of Shade (Part Five)

Werewolves of Shade (Part Six)

Moon Trilogy

Moonlight (Moon Trilogy) Book 1

Moonbeam (Moon Trilogy) Book 2

Moonshine (Moon Trilogy) Book 3

The Jack Seth Novellas

Hollow Pit (Book One)

Seeking Cara (Book Two) Coming Soon!

Black Hill Farm (Books 1 & 2)

Black Hill Farm (Book 1)

Black Hill Farm: Andy's Diary (Book 2)

Sydney Hart Novels

Witch (A Sydney Hart Novel) Book 1

Yellow (A Sydney Hart Novel) Book 2

The Doorways Saga

Doorways (Doorways Saga Book 1)

The League of Doorways (Doorways Saga Book 2)

The Queen of Doorways (Doorways Saga Book 3)

The Tessa Dark Trilogy

Stilts (Book 1)

Zip (Book 2)

The Mechanic

The Mechanic

The Dark Side of Nightfall

The Dark Side of Nightfall (Book One)

The Dark Side of Nightfall (Book Two)

Unscathed

Written by Tim O'Rourke & C.J. Pinard

You can contact Tim O'Rourke at

www.kierahudson.com or by cmail at

kierahudson91@aol.com

73669765R00143

Made in the USA
Lexington, KY
11 December 2017